Louise Jordan Miln

Quaint Korea

Louise Jordan Miln

Quaint Korea

ISBN/EAN: 9783743393332

Manufactured in Europe, USA, Canada, Australia, Japa

Cover: Foto ©Andreas Hilbeck / pixelio.de

Manufactured and distributed by brebook publishing software (www.brebook.com)

Louise Jordan Miln

Quaint Korea

CONTENTS.

CHAPTER I.

A FEW WORDS ABOUT HAMEL . .

CHAPTER II.

SOME CURIOUS KOREAN CUSTOMS .

CHAPTER III.

SÖUL FROM THE CITY WALL . .

CHAPTER IV.

KOREA'S KING . . . .

CHAPTER V.

KOREAN WOMEN . . . .

CHAPTER VI.

KOREAN WOMEN (*continued*) . .

CHAPTER VII.

KOREAN ARCHITECTURE 161

CHAPTER VIII.

HOW THE CHINESE, THE JAPANESE, AND THE KOREANS AMUSE THEMSELVES 189

CHAPTER IX.

A GLANCE AT KOREAN ART 209

CHAPTER X.

KOREA'S IRRELIGION 226

CHAPTER XI.

KOREA'S HISTORY IN A NUTSHELL . . . 245

CHAPTER XII.

THE SCOURGES OF CHINA 266

CHAPTER XIII.

JAPAN'S INGRATITUDE 278

GLOSSARY 305

QUAINT KOREA.

CHAPTER I.

A FEW WORDS ABOUT HAMEL.

A SPOILED woman, an extremely cross Englishman, who was her husband, and a smiling mandarin, who was their host, sat on the prow of a Chinese junk. They were rather a silent trio. The mandarin knew, or pretended he knew, no English. The Englishman pretended to know considerable Chinese, but, as a matter of fact, knew almost none. The two men were about equally fluent in rather bad French, and were wont to use it as the medium for a good deal of conversation, when they were alone. But to-night, with the spoiled woman sitting between them, neither seemed to have a word to say. Perhaps they both felt embarrassed by what to both of them must have seemed the ridiculousness of the situation.

The junk had left Shanghai a few days before. It was bound for Korea, where the mandarin was going on business—on business for the Emperor of China. The party on the boat, not to mention servants and such, included the mandarin, the mandarin's wife, the Englishman, the Englishman's wife, and a young man named John Stewart-Leigh.

As I have said, his excellency the mandarin was going to Korea on business. The spoiled woman was going for pleasure; her husband was going because he thought he ought to, and the mandarin's wife was going because she had to. Stewart-Leigh would probably have found it very hard to tell even himself just why he was on board. "It's as good a way of spending my leave as another, since I am too poor to go home just now," he had said to a brother subaltern in Hong Kong, "and it will be a perfect charity to Q."

Mr. Q., the spoiled woman's husband, had been stopped by a friend a few weeks before as he came down the steps of the Shanghai club.

"I say, Q.," cried the other, "what is this? I hear that you are going to Korea, and in his junk, with Ja Hong Ting. I say, it isn't true, is it?"

"Of course it's true," Q. had replied gloomily.

"That mad wife of mine has inveigled the poor old mandarin into inviting her. She insists upon going, and I am going along to chaperon her."

The Q's. had been living in China for almost a year. They had known Ja Hong Ting when he had been the Chinese minister at one of the European capitals. Indeed, an uncle of Mrs. Q.'s (she was not unmixedly English) had been the European secretary of the legation of which Ja Hong Ting had been the head. The acquaintance that had begun on the continent of Europe (and which between the then-girl and the China-man had been rather a friendly acquaintance) had developed in Pekin, as friendships between Chinese and Europeans don't often develop. Mr. Q., who alternately laughed and grumbled at his wife's odd tastes, secretly shared them. He was a grave, quiet man; as a rule, almost taciturn. He was a deal of a philosopher, though no one but his wife ever suspected it, and he had become very much interested in Ja Hong Ting and the glimpses of real China and of real Chinese life which had been afforded him through his acquaintance with the mandarin.

When Ja Hong Ting and the Q's. had first met in the drawing-room of one of the European Legations at Pekin, Ja Hong Ting had exclaimed, as he bowed over and over Mrs. Q.'s hand,

"I am so glad you are here. Now you shall know my wife." (His wife had not been with him in Europe.) " You shall teach her English, and she shall teach you Chinese. I entreat you and your husband to come to my yamun to-morrow, and there you and she shall be made great friends."

Ja Hong Ting had not spoken in English, of course.

The Q's. had gone to the yamun the next day, but Ja Hong Ting's programme had not been altogether carried out. His wife had been obedient, as most Chinese wives are, but she had taken a dislike to the Englishman, and a most violent dislike to the Englishwoman. She was civil then and afterwards (at least, in the mandarin's presence), but she never warmed to her husband's European friends, most especially not to the lady. She taught Mrs. Q. no Chinese, at least not voluntarily; and from Mrs. Q. she learned no English.

Some months after, Ja Hong Ting had called upon the Q's. in Shanghai. He stayed to dinner, and as they sat down, said to Mrs. Q., " Do you know where Korea is ? "

" Of course I know where Korea is," replied his hostess.

" Yes," interrupted Q., " so do I. It is one

of the few places that my wife has not dragged me to yet."

"Ah, yes! I forgot," said the mandarin, turning again to his hostess. "Yes, I remember, you are a great geographer and a traveller. But I do not suppose you will ever go to Korea. I should think it the last place pleasant for you to visit. I have been there a number of times, and I am going next month. The Emperor is sending me with a message to the King of Korea."

Mrs. Q. pushed her plate of untasted soup from her, and cried, "Oh!" Mr. Q. knitted his brows and sighed. He saw trouble in the distance.

"You pity me," said the mandarin.

"Pity you!" said the woman. "Ah! don't you think the Emperor would send me in your place?"

The Chinaman laughed. "I am sure his Majesty would not care to give you so much hard work to do."

"How do you get there, how are you going?" said Q., trying in a blind, groping way to turn the conversational tide.

"In my junk," said Ja Hong Ting. "It is one of the biggest junks in China—a comfortable boat, quite like a floating home, as madame here would call it, and I always enjoy my sails over to

Korea and back very much more than I enjoy my stay in Korea."

" Will any of your ladies go with you ? " asked Mrs. Q.

The mandarin laughed and shook his head. And then something seemed to occur to him. He put down the spoon that had been almost to his mouth, and after a moment's pause, said, " I could take one or two of them. There's room, and there's comfort in the boat. Would you " —turning to Q.—" like to come and bring your wife ? "

Q. groaned, and said hastily, " Thanks awfully, but I shall have to go to Calcutta next month." But as he spoke he knew that he was like a drowning man catching at a straw. The mandarin's suggestion was, of all suggestions in the world, the one to fire Mrs. Q.'s easily fired imagination.

And so it came about that a month or more afterwards Ja Hong Ting's junk had pushed off from Shanghai with " us five in family," as Mrs. Q. delightedly called the mandarin, his wife, and their three guests.

The West has conquered the East. Christianity has triumphed. Heathenism is mangled, and, led us hope, dying. Across the fair, flower-dimpled back of Asia we have laid the unpicturesque blessing of railroads, and thoroughly well-made, thoroughly well-kept paths for the men who consider life a succession of journeys, and the animals who enable such men to perpetually journey.

Second-sight seems to be, and to have always been, a genuine possession with the Asiatic peoples. We in the West have, I think, never possessed second-sight; but that does not altogether prove that there is no such thing as second-sight. I remember an Æolian harp that used to hang upon one of the crumbling, wild-flower-wreathed walls of the old castle at Heidelberg. I remember the love songs that the wind used to sing to that harp; the love songs with which the harp accepted the wooing of the wind. If a nice new organ, a parlour organ, bought on time-payment, were placed beside that Æolian harp (for I suppose the harp is still where I, in my girlhood, years ago, saw it), the wind would have nothing to say to that organ. If the wind had, the organ would not hear. I do not for a moment rank an Æolian harp above a nice, new parlour organ, but I may, perhaps, prefer the harp to the organ. We all have our secrets.

The Korean mind is, if I at all understand it, an Æolian harp. Compared with the Oriental mind,

the Occidental mind—in many instances at least—
partakes somewhat of the character of the parlour
organ.   The peoples of Asia do less than we, but I
think that they foresee more.   The wind of prophecy, the wind that prophesied the unavoidable
future, swept the nerve-strung heart of Asiatic
sensibility, swept it very many, many years ago.
And Asia, having ears to hear, and, perhaps, eyes
to see into the future, realized that her only safety
lay in seclusion.   It seems to me that the sensi-
tive Asiatic mind, the exquisitely-strung Æolian
harp of Oriental existence, sings one eminently,
practicable, sensible song into the moon-lit, star-
gemmed Asiatic midnight, and the refrain of the
song is this: "Asia for the Asians.   Mangoes
for the Chinese and the Bengalese.   Mogree
flowers for the nautch-girls; and the Taj Mahal
for the wife who was loved with a love exceeding
the love of European men."   It has, I think,
been an instinct, a second-sight, an inspiration,
with the Asiatic peoples to keep our feet from off
the flower-made brilliance of their native sod.
But we have conquered Asia, as surely as the
music pumped by the thick, red fingers of the
Board-School-taught girl—pumped from out the
well-manufactured depths of the time-payment-
bought parlour organ—would drown the inde-
finable, soft, methodless, nameless music of the

Æolian harp. Just so well have we subdued Asia, hushed her music, quenched her light, torn her flowers petal from petal.

I am speaking from the sentimental standpoint, of course. But, in this utilitarian age of ours, isn't it worth while to look at things sentimentally, once in a way, if only for variety? We have conferred the greatest practical blessings upon Asia; that I admit and maintain. But we have blurred the picture a bit, and I can't help being sorry. Only one country in Asia has, until lately, entirely escaped the blight and the blessing of our civilizing touch—Korea! Korea has not seemed worth our shot and powder. And many of us have not really known that there was such a place as Korea. But the war that is raging in farther Asia now has quickened our interest in the quaint kingdom of the morning calm.

The following chapters have been largely written from notes that Mrs. Q. made during the pleasant months she spent in Korea, and from her memories of those months. But Chosön is too interesting and, to us, too new a theme to need the fillip of any petty personality; and so, after these few pages of introduction and of explanation, we may excuse Mrs. Q., or at least her personality, from our service, and leave her in her privacy, to congratulate herself upon her good luck in having had the unique experience of seeing Korea, and of seeing it in company with one of the best-informed of Tartars, and one of the most intelligent of Europeans.

I felt impelled to write this explanation of how the material for the book was gathered, and the manner of woman who gathered it. Helen Q. lays as little claim to being profound as do I myself, and this is no volume for those who gloat on statistics, on accurate tables, and insist upon having over-exact information or no information at all. It is a peep at Korea as a very average woman saw it, a woman who enjoyed herself in Korea, and who there jotted down some of her impressions that they might serve her and another for 'sweet discourses in their time to come'—jotted them down with no dream of future publication. I sometimes think that the half-gossip of such travellers, the honest, unstudied report of their observations, gives, to the generality of readers, a more vivid, concrete picture of a strange land than do the more elaborate, more careful volumes of more accomplished writers, more professional makers of books.

These pages have had the advantage of being revised both by Mr. Q. and Ja Hong Ting, both of whom are acute observers, exact thinkers, and happen to be in Europe now.

The inclusion here of the chapters on China and Japan needs, I think, no apology. The histories of the three countries have been so interknit socially, artistically, and scientifically; the people of Korea are so like the people of Japan, so like the people of China—though so unlike both—that we shall only even partially see Korea, by keeping one of our mental eyes on the rival countries between which she lies.

The island of Quelpaert is barely fifty miles long and only half so wide; but it is big with history, huge with interest, and great with special claim upon European attention.

In 1653 a Dutch boat was wrecked on the shore of Quelpaert. To that shipwreck Europe owed her most vivid, if not her first photograph of Korea; for on the *Sparrow-hawk* was not only Min Heer Cornelius Lessen, the governor-elect of Tai-wan, but also a man of genius, a sailor who had a great gift for narrative writing. That man's name was Hendrik Hamel. It is two hundred years and more since he wrote his simple, straightforward, convincing record of the years he perforce spent in Korea. Since then some score of books have been written about Korea and things Korean. None of them are more readable than Hamel's " Narrative of an Unlucky Voyage," and only one of them compares, at all to its author's credit, with the quaint old book, written two centuries ago by the Dutch seaman.

I should like to quote a great deal of Hamel's own record of the thirteen years he spent in Korea, and it has been done very much at length by several eminent writers. Moreover, it would be an entirely safe thing to do, for the copyright must have long since run out, if the book ever had a copyright. But I will content myself with a very few words about this wonderful man and his stay in Chosön, and a few brief quotations from one of the most interesting books of travel that has ever been written; a book as fresh and readable to-day as if it had just come smoking from the printer's press.

More than half the souls on board the *Sparrow-hawk* (that is thirty-six) reached the shore of Korea. They were taken prisoners, and were held so for thirteen years and more. The history of their captivity is the history of varying kindnesses and unkindnesses. But, when we remember the then conditions of Korean life, and when we remember how little the hermit people of the hilly peninsula desired colonists, when we remember how they regarded foreigners, and what cause they had to so regard foreigners, it is more the history of kindness than of unkindness. Certainly the Hollanders had more to be thankful for than to complain of during their first years in Chosön —barring, of course, the facts that there they were and there they had to stay.

Hamel and his fellows were not the first Europeans, not even the first Hollanders to land, or rather be thrown, upon Korea. But, for all that, they were enough of rarities to be regarded by the populace as strangely interesting wild beasts. They were given rice-water to drink. They were fed. When the need came they were clad. They were sheltered. They suffered no indignity, and only comparative hardship; and, little as they dreamed it, the King of Korea was sending to them an interpreter; a man whose blood was their blood, whose tongue was their tongue.

"The first known entrance of any number of Europeans into Korea," writes Griffis, "was that of Hollanders, belonging to the crew of the Dutch ship *Hollandra*, which was driven ashore in 1627. . . . A big, blue-eyed, red-bearded, robust Dutchman, named John Wetteree, whose native town was Rip, in North Holland, volunteered on board the Dutch ship *Hollandra* in 1626, in order to get to Japan."

Now one fine day, when the *Hollandra* was coasting along Korea, Wetteree and two of his mates went ashore for fresh water. The natives caught them, and, as was the custom of the country, detained them. They were treated with respect, with honour even, attained to positions of responsibility and trust, and became great among the great men of Korea. Two of them died in 1635, died fighting for the country of their enforced adoption when she was invaded by the Manchius. But Wetteree lived on, and, twenty-seven years after his own capture, he was sent to interpret between his shipwrecked countrymen and their captors. Alas! his tongue had forgot its mother cunning, and refused to utter the language that he had not used for twenty-seven years. Wetteree remembered but a few words of Dutch. But the mother-tongue, which more than a quarter of a century had not served to make him quite absolutely forget, he regained in a month's intercourse with his countrymen.

Hamel and his comrades experienced many ups and downs. They were treated with consideration, they were treated with cruelty. They held many offices. They were set many tasks—that of begging amongst them. They plied many trades. They lived in many places. They saw the interior of Korea, the inside of Korean life, as Europeans never saw it before, and, I fancy, as Europeans have never seen it since.

Once an enterprising governor set them to making pottery with a probable view of introducing European improvements into Korea's own wonderful ceramic art methods. The experiment was a failure. Whether the Dutch fingers were ill-adapted to the pursuit of Korea's favourite art-industry, or whether, as Griffis remarks, it was "manifestly against the national policy of making no improvements on anything," history does not authoritatively tell us. I incline to the first opinion. But the bulk of the learned Europeans, who have studied Korea, certainly side with Mr. Griffis. At all events, Hamel and his fellows were not kept long at the moulding of Korean clay. The Governor was deposed and physically punished; and the Dutchmen were put to the pulling of grass from the door-yard of the palace.

Hamel and his comrades did not remain long in Quelpaert. The king sent for them and they were taken to Söul.

Two paragraphs in Hamel's long account of their stay are indicative of a good deal that is to-day as characteristic of two types of Korean character as it doubtless was two hundred years ago.

"On the 21st, a few days after the shipwreck" (writes Hamel), "the commander made us understand by signs that he wished to see all we had saved from our wreck, and that we were to bring it from our tent and lay it before him. Then he gave orders that it should be sealed up, and it was so sealed in our presence. While this was being done, some people were brought before him who had taken iron, hides, and other things that had drifted ashore from our boat. They were at once punished, and before our eyes, which showed us that the Korean officials did not mean us to be robbed of any of our goods. Each thief had thirty or more blows given him on the soles of his feet with a cudgel thick as a man's arm and tall as a man. The punishment was so severe that the toes dropped off the feet of more than one thief."

Hamel and his fellows were under the supervision of more than one governor. They were highly pleased with some, and as highly displeased with others. Here is Hamel's description of one:—" It seemed to us that he was a very sensible man, and we were afterward sure that we had not been deceived in our first opinion. He was seventy years old, had been born in Söul, and was greatly esteemed at the court. When we left his presence he signed to us that he should write to the king and ask what was to be done with us. It would be some time before the king's answer could come, because the distance was great. We begged him that we might have flesh sometimes, and other things to eat. This he granted, and he gave us leave that six of us might go abroad every day, to breathe the air, and wash our linen. This satisfied us greatly, for it was hard and weary to be shut up, and to subsist on bread and water. He also sent for us often, and made us write both in Dutch and in Korean. So did we first begin to understand some words of Korean ; and he speaking with us sometimes and being pleased to provide a little entertainment or amusement for us, we began to hope that some day we might escape to Japan. He also," adds Hamel, " took such care of us when we were sick, that we may affirm we were better treated by that idolater than we should have been among Christians."

Lest the reader should think that Hamel had become a Buddhist or a Confucist, or had adopted some other shameful form of heathenism ; lest the reader may think that Hamel was alto- gether partial to the people among whom he had been thrown, I will add what he wrote of two other governors. After complaining of one in detail, he adds, " But, God be praised, an apopletic fit delivered us from him in September following, which nobody was sorry for, so little was he liked."

And of another unsatisfactory governor he writes, " He put many more hardships upon us, but God gave us our revenge."

These last two quotations ought, I think, to establish Hamel as a highly civilized, and by no means gushing, historian.

Hamel's narrative proves two things most conclusively. It proves that of all the civilized countries the centuries have wrought the least change upon Korea. Indeed, the geological changes in the peninsula have scarcely been slower than the changes in the social customs of the Koreans. It is even more interesting to me that Hamel's book proves him one of the most truthful men who ever put pen to paper. He wrote with a brilliant, vivid pen, but he dipped it in no false colour. And yet in his own time Hamel was, to put it mildly, called a liar of liars; and until comparatively recent days his statements have been doubted, and " exaggerated " has been the least abusive adjective applied to them. But travellers of our own time, missionaries and statesmen, men whose word is beyond impugnment, testify that Hamel wrote well within the mark, that he created nothing, imagined nothing, distorted nothing. It is much to be regretted that a man who wrote of Korea so simply, so charmingly, so truthfully, and from so splendidly inside a point of view, did not write far more about a country of which the fairly well-informed of us until yesterday knew almost literally nothing; and yet a country a-teem with interest for all who feel keen interest in humanity, in art, and in high civilization, a country which threatens to disappear, if not as a country, why then, as a country apart, and whose magnificent personality may soon be lost amid the neutral generality of modern civilization, and the brotherhood (such brotherhood!) of all nations.

The history of Korea we may have always with us; but Korea—Korea of the lotus ponds and the red-arrow gates—Korea of the big hats and the devil-traps—Korea of the geisha girls and the omnipotent, red-clad king!—that we may not have so long. Civilization and war are on the march, and if 'smooth success be strewed before their gentle feet,' why then, the twentieth century in her youth may see the matrons of Chosön walk abroad unveiled, and night on the streets of Söul turned into day by electric light.

CHAPTER II.

IT is difficult to decide how to attack the study of a people of whom one knows practically nothing, and to whom one cannot have personal access.

There are two classes of travellers—of people who travel for self-gratification, and not on business or of necessity.

The traveller belonging to the first class diligently studies a whole library of guide books and other volumes of more or less tabulated, and more or less reliable information. He learns the country to which he intends journeying as he might learn his catechism or his "twelve times twelve." He buys a ticket for the land of his destination. He knows where he is going, and he goes there. He sees everything he expected to see, all he intended to see, which is all he wishes to see, and, on my word of honour, he sees no more! I know, for I have travelled with him often, oh, so often! Having worked out his own

petty educational salvation, he goes home again
almost as wise as when he started for abroad : just
a little hazed, perhaps (unless he be a globe-trotter
of the ultra rigidly-minded, blind-eyed type), for
things as they really are often give in so pro-
nounced a way the lie to things as we have read
of them, that the difference between fact and
fiction must shock all but the densest of tourists.

The traveller belonging to the second class
starts with a not too definite intention of seeing
Venezuela. He arrives there ; unless *en route* he
stumbles upon the borders of some, to him, even
more interesting country, and turns aside like the
free man he is. He rambles from town to village,
and with a mind not so crammed with information
that it has room for no more. He learns his new
country on the spot. He sees the people. He
eats their food. He drinks their wine. He
watches them at work, and at play. He learns
their language, and some of the thousand secrets
which only language can teach. He looks into
their eyes, and perchance he gets some passing
glimpse into their souls. He goes home. Then
he begins to read his guide books. Then he begins to study the history and the ancient literature
of the people among whom he has been. And
then, and not till then, is he fit to study that
history : for we can only read a history with full

intelligence if we are familiar with the people of whose ancestors it is written.

I trust that no one will think that I am decrying the study of history in our school-days, or the life-long study of those places we may not visit. I am not that mad. The study of history is invaluable as a means of mental discipline and of personal culture. But we can only get the utmost of delight, the utmost mental nourishment from history, when we are more or less (and the more the better) *en rapport* with the race whose past it chronicles.

Let us then go into Korea after the method of the second traveller, the happy-go-lucky, seemingly systemless fellow. Let us look at the Koreans of to-day. Let us peep into their houses, watch their amusements, ponder over the most characteristic of their many curious customs, and study their institutions. Then we may spend an hour or more over Korea's history, not as a duty, but a treat. Our appetites will be keen, and we shall relish what would, I am thinking, seem to us but a boredom of incomprehensible dumb dates and endless iteration of meaningless facts, were we to, after the approved style, plunge into it now!

The Koreans are, in all probability, the children of Japanese stock, but China has been for centuries their wet nurse, and their school-mistress. No two Oriental peoples are more essentially unlike than are the Chinese and the Japanese. And the Koreans, a race of Japanese, or kindred blood, living under conditions largely Chinese, and deeply imbued with Chinese ideas, present a picture peculiarly quaint, even in the quaintest part of the world.

They have Japanese faces, Chinese customs, and a manner of their own.   But into their Chinese-like customs some little Japanese habit has crept now and again.   And the Koreans have even ventured, once in a while, to invent a custom of their own.

Every Korean house has a cellar; not for the storing of wine, but for the storing of heat.   The cellar is called a khan—its mouth, through which it is fed, is some distance from the house. On a cold night you will see one or more seemingly white-clad figures cramming the khan's mouth, as fast as they can, with twigs, branches, and other combustible food.   But once well fed, the furnace burns for hours, and keeps the house warm all night.   So the attendants of the fire are not kept out in the cold over long; and while they are there, their hands are full of work that suffices to keep their blood at a decided tingle. A Korean house heated at sunset keeps warm all night, because the fire built is invariably huge, because the floors through which the heat permeates are made of oil-paper, and because the furnace itself is largely a mass of wooden and of stone intestines, pipes, and flues that retain and give out heat. With almost no exceptions the houses in Korea are one-storied. So simple a scheme of domestic architecture enables so simple a scheme of house-heating to be thoroughly efficacious.

Europeans sleeping for the first time in a Korean house, usually complain that in the middle of the night the heat is too intense, the atmosphere insupportable, and that toward the chill hours of early morning, when the fire has died, and the pipes at last grown cold, the room is most disagreeably cold. But these are minor matters, and far too trivial to disturb Korean slumber.

Next to the Eskimos, the Koreans are the heartiest eaters in the world. So, naturally enough, they sleep profoundly. They seem to be always eating. And nothing short of a royal edict, or a bursting bomb-shell, will interrupt a Korean feast. I regret to say that the flesh of young dogs is their favourite viand. Japanese beer is their favourite beverage. And for this let me commend them. For never in Milwaukee, never in Vienna, have I drank beer so good as that which is made at the Imperial brewery in Tokio. Like all other

Orientals, they devour incredible quantities of fish; herrings for a first choice. The herrings are caught in December, and are not eaten until March. Water-melons are the fruit most plentiful and most perfect in Korea. They are superb.

Potatoes were in disgrace, under the ban of a royal edict, when Ja Hong Ting took Helen to Korea. They had been introduced into the country shortly before the Q's. themselves. And their general use might have done much to alleviate the horrible famines which visit Korea with a horrible regularity. But their use and their culture were forbidden. Only in the less disciplined outskirts of the peninsula were they to be had. The mandarin used to send many miles for potatoes, and then they ate them in safety, only because of the flag that sheltered their house from the too scorching rays of the Korean sun. And it was so at all the legations.

But about the sign-posts in Korea. They are quaint, if you like! Each sign-post is shaped like an old-fashioned English coffin, and it is topped by a face; a very grotesquely painted, a very Korean, a very grinning, but for all that, a very human face. They used to rather startle Helen at first when she came round the corner of a country road, and found them smirking at her in the gruesome moonlight. But she grew used to them. For they were all alike. They all wore the countenance of Chang Sun, a great Korean soldier. Chang Sun lived one thousand, more or less, years ago. His life was devoted to the opening up of his country to the feet of his countrymen. He intersected the hills of Korea with pathways, and to-day he beams upon every Korean wayfarer from every sign-post. Beneath his beaming face you may (if you are learned enough) read his name. Beneath his name you may read to where the road or roads lead; how far the next settlement, or the next rest-house is, and one or two other items that are presumably of general interest to the Korean travelling public.

There are no inns nor hotels in Korea. But the rest-houses are neither few nor far between. A Korean rest-house is a species of dâk bungalow. It does not fill our jaded European ideas of luxury. But it answers the purpose of the Korean traveller fairly well. He can cook there; he can eat there; he can sleep there; he can buy Japanese beer there. The average Korean is a sensible fellow, and wants nothing more. No, I am wrong; he wants two things more : he wants to compose poetry, and to paint pictures. The Koreans are a nation of poets, and of painters. Every fairly educated Korean writes poems and paints pictures. But there is nothing to prevent him from doing either, or both, inside or outside the Korean rest-house. The majority of well-to-do Koreans are highly educated, as Korean education goes; and in many ways it goes very far indeed.

In Korea, as in China, a man's social position depends upon the prestige he can establish for himself at competitive examinations. In Korea, as in every other normal quarter of the globe, a woman's social position depends upon the social position of her husband.

The results of the Korean competitive examinations are said to be bribable and corruptible. Very possibly. Most human institutions are fallible. Even Achilles, you know, had a heel. But certainly Korea has been for centuries and centuries a country where scholarship took precedence of everything but kingship; a country where education was esteemed above common-sense.

All the Korean animals are very strong, but very strange. The peninsula abounds in tigers, bears, cows, horses, swine, deer, dogs, cats, wild boars, alligators, crocodiles, snakes, swans, geese, eagles, pheasants, lapwings, storks, herons, falcons, ducks, pigeons, kites, magpies, wood-cocks, and larks. Hens are plentiful, and the eggs are delicious. But the natives do not make half the use one would expect of all this feathered plenty.

Goats may be reared by no one but the king, and are exclusively used for religious sacrificial purposes.

The Koreans are good to their children, and to all animals. Snakes and serpents are, perhaps, treated by them with more veneration and tenderness than any other form of animal life. No Korean ever kills a snake. He feeds it, and does everything else he can to conduce to its comfort. The poorest and hungriest Korean will share his evening meal with the reptiles that sneak and crawl about the rocks that bound his garden.

Ancestral fire is a very important thing in Korea. In every Korean house burns a perpetual fire, which is sacred to the dead ancestors of the household. To tend that fire, to see that it never runs the least risk of going out, is the first, the most important duty of every Korean housewife. In Korea, as in China, ancestor-worship is the real religion. Confucianism is the avowed religion of the country. But, like the Chinese, the Koreans hold dogmatic religions in considerable, good-natured contempt.

Fortune-tellers and astrologers are as many and as prosperous in Korea as in China.

Like the Japanese, the Koreans have found a special and profitable vocation for their blind. In Japan, the needy blind invariably practise shampooing. In Korea, the blind exorcise devils, and, in analogous ways, make themselves generally useful. Their dealings with evil spirits are summary and thorough. The gifted blind man frightens the devil to death by means of noise more diabolical than any Satan ever heard, or catches the devil in a bottle, and carries it in triumph to a place of safety, where devils cease from troubling, and afflicted Koreans are at rest.

The laws of Korea are explicit concerning high treason. They smite it hip and thigh. They exterminate it root and branch. If a Korean is found guilty of high treason he dies, and his entire family dies with him. In this custom the Koreans are again Chinese and not altogether un-Japanese.

The constitution of the Korean Home Office is based upon the Japanese system. The Foreign Office is modelled on the Chinese Foreign Office. At the head of the War Office is the Pan Sö, or decisive signature, an official of very great power. Under him are several lesser officials called Cham Pan, or help to decide. Under these are men called Cham Wi, or help to discuss, and again under these are a number of secretaries. But alas! in the present Oriental imbroglio (although Korea is nominally the *causa belli*), the Korean War Department is playing a part so insignificant, that we do not even hear of it.

The Korean army, as estimated by the Korean War Office, represents a goodly number of men, and European writers of note have put down the militant force of the country at a million and more. But even, numerically speaking, this statement should be taken with a whole cellar of salt, and martially speaking, exaggeration could not decently go farther. The Korean army is but the shadow of an army, the harmless phantom of a force that once drove the invading Japanese armies from the shores of Chosön, and made the warriors of an American iron-clad pay dearly for their intrusion.

But if the prowess of the Korean soldiery is gone, its picturesqueness remains, and in its very inefficiency it speaks to us of the days—now probably gone for ever—when weapons at which we smile to-day were formidable indeed, the days when warfare which would excite the scorn of our school-boys was warfare grim and earnest. And as we watch that martial mockery—the army of Korea—we may realize that the yesterday of Chosön was midway between the copiously

equipped to-day of our modern, European civilization, and that primeval time when there were no
implements, the days when women used thorns
for needles, and men used thorns for fish-hooks.

Korea deals with crime as rigorously as China
does, but her methods of punishment—especially
the most cruel ones—have been borrowed from
Japan, or borrowed by Japan from Korea.   In
China, Japan, and Korea we constantly find the
same ideas, the same methods of life, with only
the slightest local differentiations, but more often
than not it is impossible for the most erudite
scholar—not to mention the casual European
wayfarer—to determine in which of the three
countries the common idea or custom was born.

Some of the customary Korean punishments
would make, I think, too painful reading : this, I
am sure, they would make too painful writing.   I
must refer the reader who is curious to Hamel ;
for Hamel details them with considerable gusto,
even the most horrible : the punishment that used
to be meted out to Korean murderers.   Happily,
even in Korea, time cures some ills, and of later
years, particularly under the rule of the present
king, a good, wise, and gentle man, the Korean
criminal code, if it has not assimilated some fraction of that quality which "is an attribute to God
Himself," has at least ceased to be the thing of

horrid cruelty it was ; and if the laws of Chosön are more pitiless than the laws of Draco, still they disgrace the humanity of Korea far less than they did two thousand years ago. I know of no other respect in which Korea has changed more.

Here are two examples of Korean law—two laws that for centuries were so rigidly carried out, that their enforcement became national customs.

" If a woman murder her husband she is to be taken to a highway on which many people pass, and she shall be buried up to her shoulders. Beside her an axe shall be laid, and with that axe all who pass by her, unless they be noble, must strike her on the head, and this none, save the noble, must fail to do, until she be dead."

There are no bankruptcy courts in Korea. A Korean who once contracts a debt can never escape from it. Here is the law :—

" One who owes money, and at the promised time fails to pay it, whether the debt be to his Majesty the King, or to another person or other persons, shall be beaten two or three times a month on the shin, and this punishment shall be continued until the debt is discharged. If a man die in debt, his relations must pay that debt, or be beaten two or three times a month on the shin."

This old law, slightly modified, still holds in Korea, I believe. Of course it works both ways. It makes it very hard for the debtor to escape payment; it makes it almost impossible for the creditor to lose any part of his substance.

CHAPTER III.

SEEN from the wall (a most wonderful wall which describes a circuit of 9975 paces), Söul looks like a bed of thriving mushrooms, mushrooms planted between the surrounding high hills, but grown in many places up on to those hills. Yes; they look very much like mushrooms, those low, one-storied houses, with their sloping, Chinese-like roofs, some tiled, some turfed, and all neutral tinted. The houses of Söul are as alike as mushrooms are, and as thickly planted.

The wall defines the city with a strange outline. Now it dips into the tiny valley, now it pulls itself up on to the top of some high hill.

Korea is a most distressingly hilly country. If you elect to go for a decent stroll, it is a matter of climbing a hill, and when you reach the summit of the hill it is a matter of tumbling down the other side, to scramble up another hill, and your path will be just such a succession of ups and downs, even though you go north until you reach the "Ever White Mountain," and, in reaching it, reach the "River of the Duck's Green," which, flowing towards the south, divides Korea from China; reach the Tu Man Kang which, flowing towards the north-east, divides Korea from the territory of the Tsar. Up and down it will be, even though you push east until you reach the purple "Sea of Japan." Still up and down you will find it, although you go as far south, or as far west, as Korea goes, and find yourself on the shores of China's "Yellow Sea." Korea looks like a stage storm-at-sea. Its hills are so many that they lose their grandeur, as individuality is lost in multitude.

But we must get back on to the wall, the wall of Söul.

The wall, which is purely Chinese in character, is punctuated by eight gates. All of them have significant names. Several of them are strictly reserved for very special purposes. The south gate is called "The Gate of Everlasting Ceremony." The west gate is "The Gate of Amiability." The east gate is "The Gate of Elevated Humanity." The south-west gate is "The Gate of the Criminals." The majority of Korean criminals, who are condemned to death, are beheaded. But this may not be within the city walls. The procession of the man about to die passes through the "Criminals' Gate." And that gate is never opened save on the occasions of such gruesome functions. The south-east gate is "The Gate of the Dead." No corpse is interred within the city walls. And no corpse, save only the corpse of a king, may pass through any other gate than the "Gate of the Dead." Any corpse (but the monarch's) would defile the gates through which Söul's humanity is wont to ebb and flow. The "Gate of the Dead" has another name. It is often called "The Gate of Drainage," for by its side the River Hanyang flows out to the Yellow Sea. The northern gate stands high upon the summit of a peculiarly shaped hill, which the French missionaries aptly named "Cock's Comb." This gate is never opened save to facilitate the flight of a Korean king.

The gates differ greatly in size, which adds to the unusual picturesqueness of the wall.

The Cock's Comb, up to whose highest ridge the wall of Söul runs, is at once the most distinct and the most interesting bit of Söul's background. It is, among the mountains of the world, so uniquely shaped that no one who has ever seen it can ever forget it. And it is the altar of the most sacred of Korea's national ceremonies.

Although a large portion of this hill is enclosed

within Söul's wall, Söul itself, climbing city though it is, has not climbed far up the hill. The summit of the Cock's Comb is an uninhabited, high suburb of Söul.

When the night has well fallen, when the " white " clad masses in Söul's market-place can no longer see the outlines of the hill, four great lights break out upon that hill's crest. To all in Söul those lights cry out, " All's well. In all Korea, all's well." Each light represents two of the eight provinces into which Korea is divided. If in any Korean province or county there is war, or threatening of war, a supplementary light burns near the light that indicates that province. If the war-light is placed on the left, war or invasion threatens one province, if the war light is placed on the right, war or worse threatens another province.

The bonfire signal service of the Korean War Office is complicated and elaborated. One extra fire means that an enemy has been sighted off some part of the sandy Korean coast. Two lights mean that the enemy have landed ; three mean the enemy are moving inland ; four mean they are pushing toward the capital ; five—! Well, when five such fires flare up, the citizens of Söul can only pray—or run and drown themselves in the rapid rushing river that leaves Söul as the condemned leave it—because those five bonfires mean that the enemy draw near the city's gate.

Telegraphy—as Edison knows it—is unknown in Korea. But the Koreans have a weird but vivid telegraphy of their own.

At short intervals upon their rocky, sandy coast huge cranes are built. Each crane is tended by a trusted official of the Korean king. When dusk begins to fall, the attendant of the crane lights in it a great bonfire, if all is well. That bonfire's light is seen by the attendant of a fire some miles more inland—some miles nearer Söul—and so from every pace of Korea's boundary, the faithful servants of Korea's king flash to Korea's capital the message, "All is well." A hundred lines of message-light meet upon that queer hill, the " Cock's Comb " of Söul.

Many a night of late, unless the wires have lied to us, there must have been a great confusion among those signal fires, and vast confusion in poor frightened Söul.

A certain light will mean " China has pounced upon us." Another light will mean " Japan has stabbed us." And a score of other lights will mean a score of dire facts which only the heads of the Korean War Department could translate for us, if they would.

Curfew shall not ring to-night. " Ah! how

often," said Helen, when this Chino-Japanese war was first declared, " I have seen those four placid bonfires tell the gentle Koreans that no Lion of England nor of India had roared, that no Eagle of Russia (not to needlessly mention Austria or America) had swooped, no dragon of China or Japan had belched destroying fire! To-night, if those fires burn, they flash a message of dire distress to Söul's shrinking, blue-robed men, and hidden, unseen women, unless happily they are unconscious what an excuse for war their isolated peninsula has become."

Poor Korea! what has she done? Nothing unwomanly. But womanlike she has been unfortunately situated.

China has just suffered a plague.

Japan has just suffered an earthquake. For very many years China and Japan have thought it expedient to soothe national heart-ache (resultant upon national disaster) with the potent mustard plaster of war.

The Chinese hate the Japanese. The Japanese hate the Chinese. The Koreans hate the Japanese and the Chinese, and are hated by both. An Oriental imbroglio is not hard of conception.

The worst of it is that Korea seems doomed. And Korea, with all her faults, is one of the few. remaining widows of the dead (but not childless) old world. And she, good purdah-woman that she is, is lying down with considerable wifely dignity upon the funeral pile, which civilization has lit to cremate the false, old notions of the past.

One who has lived in Korea can but think it rather a pity that Korea should cease to be, or be too much remodelled, whoever's in the wrong— Japan or China.

Nature has found Korea so nearly perfect, that it seems almost profane for man (or those combinations of men called nations) to find fault with her. In Korea there are snows that never melt. In Korea there are flowers that never cease to bloom.

The land of the morning calm! Poor little peninsula (only twice and a half the size of Scotland), the soft, rosy Oriental haze is going to be ripped off of you, and in the cold, clear, brilliant light of Westernized day you are going to fade away into nothing! But before you quite fade away let us have a peep at you. You are superior in many ways to our land. For one thing, you begin your year more sensibly. You ring the new year in with the birth of the year's first flowers.

The Korean new year is a month later than ours. The snow is still upon the ground there in

February. But even so, the fruitless plum-trees open their myriad buds, and long before the cold snow has melted from their feet, their heads are covered with a warm, tinted, perfumed snow of bloom. A few weeks later, and the cherry trees are white with a magnificence of blossom that nowhere in this world cherry-trees can excel, not even in Japan. Before the cherry blossoms fall the wisteria breaks into ten thousand clusters of purple loveliness. Then the peonies flaunt in every fertile and half fertile spot, and mock, like the impudents they are, the splendour of the sun. But their proud heads fall ere long, and all Korea is lovely with the iris.

Autumn is the most delightful of the Korean seasons. It is matchless. Not even on the banks of the Hudson does summer die so splendid a death as she dies in Korea. The Korean summer, superb and perfumed as she is, is very like that false Cawdor of whom Malcolm said to Duncan :

> "Nothing in his life
> Became him like the leaving it."

Winter in Korea is unqualifiedly cold. The hills are white with snow, and the rivers are grey with ice. The people huddle into their over-heated houses. And I believe that the entire nation does not own a pair of skates. The only sleds, or sleighs, belong to the fishermen who crack through the ice to catch their finny prey. The fisherman sits upon the sled as he plies his noiseless industry, and when his day's work is done he piles his scaly plunder upon the sled, and so drags it to the market-place.

But it was summer when Helen first stood upon the wall of Söul. A parapet crenulates the outer edge of that old wall. It is broken with loopholes, and notched with embrasures. And every few yards its broken outline is broken again by the overhanging branches of flower-heavy trees, or by the bright blossoms of some vine that has found root in one of the old wall's mossy niches.

And within this picturesque wall huddles superlatively picturesque Söul.

The royal palaces are noticeable for their gardens and their size. Big as they are, and they are very big, they are none too big for the vast harem that forms a most important part of their household.

Far from the houses of the king stands " The South set Apart Palace." The resident Chinese Commissioner lived there. In front of this building stands one of Söul's two remarkable " Red Arrow. Gates." Near is the United States legation.

One of the most interesting features of Söul is

its little Japanese colony. The following description of it was written a few years ago by a talented American, who was for some months the guest of the king of Korea :—

" With its back up against the South Mountain stands the building of the Japanese legation. From a flagstaff above it floats the Japanese ensign, the red ball on the white field. Here lives the little Japanese colony, a true bit of transplanted Japan, all alive in an alien land. Some of the legation have with them their wives, and many children play about the courtyard.

" It has its own force of soldiers, kept constantly recruited from home; its doctors, its policeman— all it can need to be sufficient to itself. The minister is as much a governor as a representative at a foreign court. Day and night the soldiers stand before the gateway of the legation building and change guard as if it were a camp; and whenever the minister goes abroad a certain number of them accompany him as escort. The soldiers are needed. Twice the legation has had to fight its way from Söul to the sea."

In Korea when one dynasty gives way to another (and that is a fairly frequent occurrence) the newly-throned dynasty abandons the capital of the old dynasty and establishes for itself, and its heirs for ever, a new capital. So was Söul established five hundred years ago by the first crowned ancestor of Korea's present king.

The city wall was thrown about a very considerable area. And according to rigid Korean custom, that wall must for ever mark the city's limits. But the actual city, the city of the people, has surged far beyond that wall.

One class of Söul's inhabitants—a most important class—lives almost in its entirety outside the city's gates. The fishermen of Söul live in the river suburbs. There they ply their trade winter and summer; and, I might almost add, day and night. They live upon the banks of the river from which they draw their livelihood. Their quaint low houses fringe the edge of the land, and their boats fringe the edge of the water.

Fish and rice are the staple foods of the Koreans, save in the north of the peninsula, where rice will not grow. There fish and millet are the general food. Fish is the great staple throughout the country. And no class of men, perhaps, are so important to Söul's general welfare as the fishermen who live just beyond the walls, and daily come into her market-places to sell their slippery spoil. Meat is scarcely eaten in Korea. Korea is a land of fearful famines. The rice fails. The millet fails. Everything fails except the fish. Yes; I think that I may unqualifiedly say, that to Korea no class is so important as the fishermen—to the very life of the Koreans no class so necessary, so indispensable.

The women of position are carried through the streets in the closest of closed palanquins. A woman of the middle class, if obliged to walk abroad, invariably wraps an ordinary dress about her head and shoulders. And very far from seductive does she look. The long loose sleeves of the dress hang from her head like great, ungainly, shapeless ears. And the folds of the ungraceful garment are held tightly in front of her face by one determined hand—a hand that never does, and for nothing in the world would, relax its hold. The women of the very poorest class, the hewers of wood and drawers of water, are indeed compelled to, with uncovered heads and unveiled faces, go about the streets. But they move rapidly. They look neither to the right nor to the left. And they slink by men with downcast eyes. And men never look at them. Indeed a Korean gentleman will not, by one single glance, betray that he is aware of the presence in public of any woman; unless indeed she belong to the geisha, or "accomplished class." The geisha girls go about the streets frankly, and unhiddenly enough. But they are a class aside.

In Korean wifehood, in Korean motherhood, they have no part.

The Koreans take a great deal of medicine —those that can afford it—and it never seems to do them any harm. For the rich, pills of incredible size are richly gilded and placed in elaborate boxes. The poor take smaller pills ungilded, and omit the boxes altogether. Very many Koreans take medicine at regular intervals without the slightest reference to their then state of health. These systematic persons do not take medicine when they are ill, unless the illness has the good taste to fall upon their duly appointed medicine-day. This is how an old Korean explained to Helen the philosophy of the medicine-regularly-taken theory. "On every seventh day you rest whether you are tired or not. And on all the other days you work, whether you are tired or not. So do we take our medicine, once in so many weeks, because it is well to observe system : to be regular." The old man's eye twinkled finely as he spoke, as who should say, "What are you answered now?" And Helen rather felt that he had her on the hip.

Mr. Percival Lowell says : "In Korea, medicine is an heirloom from hoary antiquity. An apothecary's shop there needs not to adorn itself with external and irrelevant charms, like the beautiful purple jar that so deceived poor little

Rosamond. Upon eminent respectability alone it bases its claim to custom ; and its traditions are certainly convincing. Painted upon suitable spots along the front of the building runs the legend, " *Sin Nong Yu Öp*,"—that is, "the profession left behind by Sin Nong." This eminent person was a " spiritual agriculturist," the discoverer of both agriculture and medicine ; and the pills sold in the shops to-day are supposed to be the counterparts of those invented by him. Worthily to render the legend, we ought to translate it, " Jones, successor to Æsculapius."

There are two distinct Koreas, distinct though having much in common : the Korea of the upper classes, and the Korea of the populace. We have of late been hearing quite a good deal about the history of Korea, about the topography of Korea, about the King of Korea, and about the Korea of the upper classes. But about the lower classes we have heard comparatively little. The literature at our disposal concerning Korea is more than meagre. Very little of this literature deals with the people—the common people of Korea.

The streets of Söul—the streets upon whose edges the people of Söul live, the streets through which the people of Söul surge—are very wide, Most of them have, however, the appearance of being very narrow. Wide streets seem to the Korean mind unnecessary luxuries. The people of Söul utilize the streets of their city by erecting temporary booths outside their houses, and beyond the booths they spread their trays and mats of merchandise. Inch by inch the street disappears beneath the extemporized shops of the people, until at last just enough room is left for the interminable procession of humanity to squeeze through. This encroachment is taken good-naturedly enough by everyone. The people positively pick their slow way between trays of nuts and mats of grain, booths of hats and sleds of fish. When the king wishes to take a promenade or ride through any of the streets of Söul, all the booths are taken from those streets, and with the trays and mats are tucked out of sight. The streets are swept and garnished. The next day, or, if it is not too late, when his Majesty has returned to his palace, the booths are re-erected, the mats and trays are re-arranged, and the every-day life of Söul goes placidly on until the sovereign elects to take another airing.

It is a common blunder to speak of the people of Söul as wearing white garments; a blunder, or rather a laziness to which I must plead guilty. Korean garments are invariably of a peculiar, delicate blue, unless the wearer be a person of much importance : then, indeed, may his garments brighten into deeper blue, flush into soft and lovely pink, or, if they chance to be the vestments of the King, blush into proudest scarlet. Seen from a distance an ordinary Korean appears to be clad in white, the blue of his dress is so pale ; and so, many careless writers—I among them—have made the mistake of saying that white is the hue of the dress of the Korean populace.

The Koreans have a passion for rugged scenery —but then, indeed, they have a passion for every manner of scenery. They call the rocks the earth's bones. They call the soil the earth's flesh. The flowers and the trees they call her hair. There is no more rugged bit of scenery near Söul than the Valley of Clothes ; and in it stands a picturesque little temple, which was built, so the Koreans say, to commemorate a battle, that they once won. It is a very beautiful specimen of Korean architecture. Indeed, I know no lovelier example of what the architecture of older Korea has become under the influence of Chinese thought and Chinese art.

Through the Valley of Clothes runs a long, clear stream, on whose banks are innumerable large, smooth-topped rocks. Altogether it is an admirable place for Oriental washing. In the winter every Korean garment is ripped into all its

component parts before it is washed. In summer
the garments are washed each in its entirety.
This ripping up of the clothes before washing
them is one of the comparatively few customs
which the Koreans have borrowed from the
Japanese. In Japan, however, all clothes about to
be washed are taken to pieces, whether it be
winter or summer.

Nothing could well be simpler than the *modus
operandi* of the Korean washermen and washerwomen. The clothes are well soaked in the
stream. Then they are well beaten with smooth,
heavy, edgeless sticks. Then they are spread upon
the ground or on the rocks, as much in the sun as
possible, and left to dry indefinitely. No one ever
steals them ! Think of it ! And even the gentle
winds of the Asiatic heavens scorn to blow them
away. If there seems the slightest chance of such
a catastrophe, a few smooth pebbles are laid upon
the garments' edges.

The qualities which the upper classes of Korea
have most in common are—love of art and literature, reverence for law, kindness of disposition, and
love of nature. The point upon which they most
differ is religion. Korea is really a country without religion. The upper classes are intellectual
to a degree, but their intellectuality is invariably
of the agnostic order. Rationalism and agnosticism

are the only recognized religions in upper Korean circles.

The Korean populace also profess agnosticism, but do not practise it; at least they do not practise rationalism; for if they believe in no gods, most of them believe in countless devils.

The sacred devil-trees are supposed to be (after the blind) most efficacious in ridding the land of the spirits of evil. A writer—one of the best writers on Korea—thus describes a devil-tree upon which he came one bleak autumn day:—"An ancient tree, around whose base lies piled a heap of stones. The tree is sacred; superstition has preserved it, where most of its fellows have gone to feed the subterranean ovens. It is not usually very large, nor does it look extremely venerable, so that it is at least open to suspicion that its sanctity is an honour which is passed along from oak to acorn or from pine to seed: however, it is usually a fair specimen of a tree, and, where there are few others to vie with it, comes out finely by comparison: otherwise there is nothing distinctive about the tree, except that it exists,—that it is not cut down and borne off to the city on the back of some bull, there to vanish in the smoke. On its branches hang, commonly, a few old rags, evidently once of brilliantly-coloured cloth; they look to be shreds of the garments of such unwary travellers as approached too close; but a nearer inspection shows them to be tied on designedly. The heap of small stones piled around the base of the tree gives one the impression at first that the road is about to undergo repairs, which it sadly needs, and that the stones have been collected for the purpose. This, however, is a fallacy: no Korean road ever is repaired.

The spot is called Son Wang Don, or "The Home of the King of the Fairies." The stones help to form what was once a fairy temple, now a devil-jail; and the strips of cloth are pieces of garments from those who believed themselves possessed of devils, or feared lest they might become so. A man caught by an evil spirit exiles a part of his clothing to the branches of one of these trees, so as to delude the demon into attaching there."

We have tried to peep at Söul—the Söul of the people. But not all Söul is plebeian. It has a most decided aristocracy, both architectural and human.

Söul has no temples. None may be built within her walls. Of all civilized countries, Korea is the one country without a religion. Religion or its analogous superstitions are there, of course; but that religion is in Korea, not part of Korea. In Korea, religion is under a ban of official discountenance, or national discredence. Such temples as do exist in Korea dwell (like architectural lepers) without the city's walls. But Söul has her official buildings, and the dwellings of her rich. Above all, she has her palaces.

But hold! there is one temple within the walls of Söul; but it is there on sufferance, there against the law. And it is just inside the walls. It is on a high, lonely mountain place, and far remote from the actual city—the throbbing, breathing, human city.

And Söul has also what was once a temple. It is as interesting as anything in Söul. In the first place it is the only pagoda in Söul—almost, if not quite, the only pagoda in Korea. In the second place, it is extremely beautiful. In the third place, it, more than any building I know, accents the decay of all things human, even of (those perhaps greatest of all human things) great thought-systems.

Yesterday—the yesterday of five hundred years ago—this, Söul's one pagoda, was a Buddhist temple. To-day it is a neglected, unconsidered, tolerated, rather than admired, ornament, in a middle-class Korean's back yard.

The pagoda of Söul owes its solitary, but not honoured, old age to the fact that unlike most pagodas of its period and kind, it was built of stone. It has eight stories (representative of eight stages or degrees of the Buddhist heaven); but it is entirely composed of two pieces of stone. In idea it is Chinese; but its form is a modification or a local adaptation of its idea; and it is peculiarly rich in most exquisite Korean carvings.

After the pagoda—perhaps before the pagoda—there are in Söul three buildings, more than any others indicative of the difference between Söul the old and conservative, and Söul the new and iconoclastic—I mean the Foreign Office, the War Office, and the Home Office. They are all of recent date, all concessions to a cosmopolitanism, with which Korea, the old, had no sympathy, and into which (though ever so little) Korea, the new, has been forced by that most brutal of all forces—the force of circumstances—forced by the irresistible might of the gigantic disproportion, to her own, of alien numbers. A few years ago Korea had never had a Foreign Office, because Korea had never deigned to be cognizant of the existence of any foreign power. True she has, for many years, paid a lazy tribute to China, and plied a lazier trade with Japan; but until a short time ago she has been essentially, and indeed, a hermit nation. Yes, it was verily the land of the morning calm. No *réveil* broke its early morning slumber; no drum woke its night to alarm. It was a heaven of earthly peace, a heaven in which there was neither fighting nor dying in battle.

But that is changed. So far as outside turmoil can ripple the placid waters, upon which the lotus-flower blooms and bends, in a luxury of perfumed sleep, as it does nowhere else—the lakes and ponds of Korea!

Korea admitted, gracefully, if enforcedly, foreigners to her shores—admitted them for purposes of commerce and of peace. Alas, she has had to recognize them as ambassadors of war, introducers of bloodshed.

Korea's army has for many years been very purely artistic, ornamentally belligerent—nothing more. It has been found impossible to evolve it into anything more brutal, nineteenth-centuryish, effective, and up-to-date.

Korea's War Office is an unhappy, if seemingly necessary, farce. It has existed for centuries. But only the conjunction, or rather the juxtaposition, of Korea with other nations has made it ridiculous.

Korea's Home Office sprang up—as it must have done in any self-respecting soil—as soon as a Foreign Office became a regrettable *fait accompli*. Until Korea had a Foreign Office, Korea's War Office was by no means the sad

burlesque that it is now. Until Korea had a
Foreign Office, she had not the filmiest need of a
Home Office. Korea was all in all to Korea.
Every effort of her being was undivertedly
directed to the welfare of herself and her own.
She had no need of, no excuse for, a Home
Office, because all was home, everything for home.
But when she was physically forced to admit
the existence of other peoples, she was morally
forced to insistently emphasize the existence of
her own people.

Söul is rich in palaces ; very rich in their quality,
if not in their quantity. Each palace is, like every
considerable Korean dwelling, a collection of
houses. And every Korean palace—like every
Korean dwelling of any distinction—is more
remarkable, more admirable because of its surroundings—its garden—than because of itself.

There are four nations pre-eminent for landscape gardening—pre-eminent in this order :—
the Japanese, the Koreans, the Chinese, the
Italians.

Korea is, by her climate, held behind Japan in
landscape gardening. Most of the flowers that
in Japan bloom all the year round, can in Korea
only bloom for a few months.

But in one phase of landscape gardening—(the
art of bringing Nature into a garden, and there

ornamenting her, without insulting her)—the Koreans quite equal the Japanese.

Water, in the form of miniature lakes, is the crown—the centre of every far-eastern garden. Nowhere in the world are artificial lakes or ponds so perfected, so ablush with bloom, so aquiver with perfume, as they are in Korea. Sometimes they dot great green swards. Sometimes they softly ripple against the very foundations of a palace; oftenest they are the one blessed detail of a middle-class man's dwelling. But they are almost always emerald with lotus-leaves, and in season, brilliant with the bloom, and fragrant with the breath of the lotus-flowers. Marble bridges span them, if they are in the king's gardens; a unique island centres them wherever they are—a wee island that is shaded by its one drooping tree. There the master of the garden spends the long summer days, basking in the surrounding beauty, smoking, drinking tea, and fishing.

CHAPTER IV.

KOREA'S KING.

It has been with genuine indignation that I have recently read that the King of Korea is weak of mind and weak of character.

Statements could scarcely have less foundation. Journalism is indeed an exacting profession, and the pressman who would wield an up-to-date pen must, once in a way, write glibly upon a subject of which he knows nothing, or less than nothing. But surely, if one chooses for one's theme a person whom one has never seen, and of whom one knows nothing authentically, the least one can, in common decency, do is to speak good, not evil of that person. If it is necessary to clothe persons of momentary interest with attributes that are wholly a fabric of guess-work, it seems to me that the most reckless scribbler is in honour bound to clothe the involuntary human lay-figure with whole, clean, garments of praise, and not with grimy rags of fantastic criticism.

As a matter of simple fact, Li-Hsi, the King of Korea, is an admirable man. He has most of the good qualities, and very few undesirable ones.

He has an exceptionally sweet nature. He has a heart of gold. He is patient, forgiving, persevering and hard-working. He is a man of decided mental strength, and of most considerable learning. The welfare of his people has been his unintermittent aim ; and to-day he is staunchly enthroned in the hearts of those people.

It has been said that his Korean Majesty is a man of contemptible personal habits. And, worst of all, it has been said that he is entirely under his wife's thumb. There is in all Christendom no monarch more sober, more unselfish than Li-Hsi. As for the last accusation, it is the one in which there is, I fear, a grain of truth. But what of it ? The same thing was said of Frederick the Good. Was he weak-minded, morally corrupt ? The same thing is said to-day (and not without some show of truth) of the Emperor of Germany, the King of Italy, and was said of the late Tsar of Russia. They are rather a wholesome, brainy, manly trio, aren't they ?

Unquestionably the Queen of Korea has great influence over the King. But surely even a king might commit a graver crime than that of being fond of his wife. For instance, he might be fond of someone else's wife. Now that strikes me as rather worse form than the other. And certainly it is the more apt to lead to deeply dire results. On the whole, I think the King of Korea might almost be forgiven his one weakness—a weakness for his own wife.

Of civilized sovereigns, the King of Korea is rather uniquely placed. No monarch could have more absolute power in his own kingdom, no monarch could well have less influence abroad. Indeed even the King's power at home seems rather tottery just now. But it has been shaken by the rough hands of alien invaders, not by the disloyal hands of his own subjects. To-day, when in Korea all is confusion and dismay, Li-Hsi is as absolutely king over the Koreans as he was when he ascended the throne thirty years ago.

His Majesty is rather under the average of Korean height, and is about forty years of age. The Queen, contrary to the usual custom in Korea, is much younger.

He wears a dress somewhat resembling the ordinary Korean court dress; but his dress is of brilliant scarlet. The dresses of his nobles are of pale .blue or pink. The King wears the usual white Korean collar, and a plastron, and shoulder pieces (or epaulettes) of gold and jewels.

All Korean hats are wonderful. A Korean

court hat is simply marvellous. It is most noticeable for its wings or ears, which project sharply
out from either side. They typify human ears,
and signify that the wearer has his ears wide
spread to catch the most whispered command of
his Majesty. Even Li-Hsi wears a court hat. But
his ears (I mean his hat's ears) stand erect, or are
at the tips caught together at the top of the hat.
This is because the Emperor of China is too far
away for his actual voice to be heard by the Korean
King, and no other human being but the Chinese
Emperor may speak to Li-Hsi with anything even
approaching insistent emphasis. To no other voice
need the King of Korea listen, unless he like. So
at least it was until a few months ago.

The King of Korea has a gracious but dignified
bearing. His face is fine and beautiful, and his
smile is peculiarly sweet and winning.

There are two great palaces in Söul: the Old
Palace and the New Palace. The New Palace is
four hundred years old and more. The old palace
is as old as Söul. The present King of Korea
lives in the New Palace. His Majesty deserted
the Old Palace, or, to be more exact, upon his
accession to the throne, declined to adopt it as his
residence, because it was full of, to him, painful
family reminiscences.

The Old Palace is one of the few Architectural

wonders of Söul. It is deserted now, and in parts decaying. It is surrounded by an admirable wall. ' Its principal gate is guarded by two gigantic stone monsters. The Koreans call them Chinese Lions, and the Japanese call them Korean dogs. They look as much like one as the other. They are of Chinese descent. The Koreans copied them from the Chinese. In Korea they caught the quick Japanese fancy. From that day they have played a conspicuous part in Japanese art, and have even become familiar to European eyes, because they grin at us from so many thousands of the cheaper (so called) Satsuma vases.

The Old Palace is a vast collection of buildings, of court-yards, of landscape gardens, of parks and of lotus-ponds. In its centre stands the famous Audience Hall, which I am almost tempted to call one of the architectural wonders of the world. I may safely call it one of the architectural and artistic wonders of Korea. Many steps lead up to the entrance of the Audience Hall. This alone is in Korea a great distinction. Save the King only, no Korean may build or own a building outside of which there are more than three steps. Four steps would be high treason, and would cost their owner a traitor's death.

In the background of the Old Palace is Nam San, the mountain upon which signal-fires burn every nightfall, telling the inhabitants of Söul that all goes well throughout the kingdom. Or if, as now, aught goes ill, the fires tell that—tell it with considerable detail. It is a curious signal-code, as complicated as ingenious; but it is beautifully vivid and altogether effective.

The New Palace is in a collection of palaces. Like Söul its grounds are surrounded by an elaborate wall. Those grounds cover over a hundred acres, every rod of which is beautiful. They are carefully laid out, but not with foolish elaborateness. Nature is accented in those palace grounds, but never interfered with. Wherever an exceptionally pretty bit of view is to be seen, there is a quaint Korean summer-house. And as the pretty bits tread upon each other's heels, the grounds are rather thick with odd summer-houses, and still odder pavilions. The Koreans are intensely fond of Nature; but they are not fond of exercise. They like to sit, even when they look upon the trees, the flowers, the hills, the sky, the lotus-ponds that they so love. Therefore the grounds of a king's house would be most incomplete, were not rest and shelter available at every few yards.

A summer-house in the grounds of the New Palace is a favourite haunt of the present king. On a drowsy summer afternoon his Majesty sits there for hours, sipping tea and watching the changeless loveliness of the view.

The Koreans drink tea almost as perpetually as the Siamese do, and, like the Siamese, they are greatly addicted to drinking it out of doors. But this must be with them a comparatively new fashion, for Hamel and many other old historians tell us that tea is seldom drunk in Korea.

To one versed in Korean architecture, it is a simple thing to distinguish the house of a king from that of a subject. The columns of the monarchs' houses are round, and their rafters are square. Only a king may use the round column or the square rafter. Only a king might, until recent years, paint his house. Only a king may wear a coat of brilliant red. Of all men, only the king may look upon the faces of the Queen's hundreds of attendant ladies. On occasions of ceremony when the King is present, only he may face the south.

The Korean soldiers are clad in dark blue relieved with crimson, and fantastically decorated with ribbons. The Chinese character which signifies valour is elaborately embroidered over their hearts. They're rather fine-looking fellows, but their manners are mild, and they impress the impartial European observer as staunch lovers of peace. They wear no helmets, but their headgear is most distinguished.

There is no other inanimate thing so important

to the Korean mind as are hats. The hat of the King is his crown. The hat of the soldier is his helmet. And no Korean owns any other chattel so valuable, so indicative of his station, state, and worth, so indispensable, so cherished as his hat; no, not even his children, never to mention his wife.

Black is the Korean hat colour. But even Korean rules have their exceptions. The hats of the Korean army officers are vivid of hue, and heavy with feathers and ribbons; and the hats of the private soldiers have at least a band or border of red to show that the wearers are men of bloodshed and fearless.

In Söul there are military hat stores galore; and naturally enough, for his hat is the most important item of the Korean soldier's uniform. As for his accoutrements, they are so completely overshadowed by the brim of his mighty hat that they shrink into unconsidered insignificance.

But in years gone by Korea's army was far less a force of straw and of plumage. The Korean eagle could shriek once—now she seems to have become metamorphosed into a military owl; blind at day, timid at night.

The military force of Korea was at an early period divided into three distinct branches: the navy, the secular army, and the armed or military monks.

The armed monks garrisoned castles and fortresses which were usually inaccessibly placed, or, as we should say to-day, built on commanding positions. They, as a rule, hung frowningly on the rough side of some steep mountain, or punctuated menacingly some narrow and difficult or treacherous pathway.

These religious warriors did not go far upon the war-path. They defended the strongholds, which were also their monasteries, and they engaged valiantly enough in local warfare. These were the most efficient and most esteemed of old Korea's soldiers. Each town furnished a required number of these holy militaries. They were officered by men of their own order. When they reached the age of sixty they retired from active service, and their sons filled up their vacant places; for they were not celibates, these warrior priests of old Chosön.

Each Korean province is under arms one year out of seven. The selected soldiers of the province (in Korea, warriorship is a matter of the king's selection, not of the soldier's election) are equipped, robed, drilled, paraded, and made generally presentable upon the picturesque, flower-dotted, and bloodless battle-fields of Korea's martial pageantries.

They take their turns in going up to Söul, these impromptu, but for all that, well-rehearsed fighting men. When they get to Söul they there invariably act well their parts. The beginning and the end of their duty are included in ceremonial functions ; and the breath of ceremony is the only air that can fully inflate the lungs of any self-respecting Asian. " No man is a hero to his own valet," we say lightly. But the peoples of the Orient take the great truth of this adage very seriously, almost grimly. They realize that the only divinity that can really hedge a king from the degrading familiarity of his subjects is the divinity of purple and fine linen, the blare of trumpets. In brief, the people (in Asia or in Europe) love a show, and the king who would sit staunchly enthroned upon the hearts, not to mention the intellects, of his people, must be followed by a train of supers as long, and as splendidly clad, as well-trained—and perhaps as meaningless—as those who make the pit of a London theatre appreciate the more clearly the regal glory of Henry the Eighth, of Arthur the deceived, and of that other Henry with whom Becket quarrelled.

But in Korea's martial comedy there are actors who are never out of the bill. Over each province a general presides, who has under him from three to six colonels ; each colonel is the military

master of several captains; each captain is the
Mars of a city, a castle, a town, or some other
fortified place.   Even the Korean villages are pro-
tected (Japan and China, save the mark!) by a
corporal.   Under the corporal are petty officers;
under the petty officers are soldiers, so-called.

There is one admirable thing about the Korean
army.   Its books are well kept, and the King of
Korea can always tell to the moment how many
fighting men are at his disposal.   If only they
could fight!   Or, if only they had no need to
fight!

Bows and arrows are conspicuous among the
implements of the Korean army.   They make
little or no impression upon the cannon of civilization, but they serve to remind us of the days
when man needed to contend but against nature,
to slaughter only birds and four-footed mammals.

The Korean infantry and the Korean cavalry
are very similarly equipped.   They wear brilliant,
if vulnerable, breast-plates.   They carry swords
nice of shape, if dull of edge, and they used, in
battles of great moment, to replace their crimson-
decked hats with head-pieces of cotton-batting and
tinsel.

There is a unique branch of the king's immediate servitors.   We should bluntly call them

spies. The Koreans picturesquely call them "messengers on the dark path." The King of Korea does not hang about the doorways, nor prowl into the back-yards of his subjects, but in every Korean city he has several, and in every Korean village at least one appointed listener. European history tells us that more than one European monarch has disguised himself at night, and held up his thirsty ears to the nectar or the gall of his subjects' candid opinions of himself. Whether eaves-dropping is more admirable when performed in person or when deputed to the hireling, is a nice question for those who would judge between East and West. It seems to me that the King of Korea does a dirty thing with rather more dignity than did Napoleon or Nero. At all events, the plebeian spies of Korea are an acknowledged branch of Korean officialism, and every Korean knows that his house, and all it contains, is very possibly under the *espionnage* of the million eyes of the king.

Korea is as netted day and night with the spies of the king as she is at night netted with signal fires. Just such a system of official *espionnage* used to exist in Japan. Did Japan copy Korea? Did Korea copy Japan? Again we ask the question, and again Asia declines to answer.

The spies of Li-Hsi are the father confessors of

the Koreans, and the custom is so old, so authentic, so much a matter of course in Korea, that the Korean caught in the utterance of treason, or relating some petty offence, cries "*mea culpa*" rather devoutly.

Not very many years ago there were in Asia three absolute monarchs with comparatively small kingdoms. Those kingdoms were Burmah, Siam, and Korea. Theebaw, the master of many wooden cannon, the monarch of Mandalay, the master of Burmah, has accepted his defeat with a good deal of dignity, and Burmah the old, Burmah the real, is fast passing off of the face of our earth.

Siam, when Sir Harry Parkes first went there, was possibly the most picturesque kingdom in Asia; but the King of Siam is a man so wise in his generation, that we may almost venture to call him a monarch up-to-date. 'Since he cannot die at the head of his elephant-cavalried army; since he cannot see that army victorious in the land of its birth and its training, he lays bits of his sword (in the form of goodly scraps of his kingdom) at the feet of French democracy, I mean republicanism.'

Theebaw is banished, and Chulalongkorn compromises. And what of Li-Hsi? This, at least, he has made the longest and most hopeless fight of them all against the inroads of Western civilization.

There is no high office in Korea, civil or military, that can be bestowed without the king's sanction, or that cannot be revoked at the king's pleasure.

Unfortunately, Li-Hsi has to take the word of the men whom he trusts, as to the efficiency of the majority of the men whom he appoints to positions of power. Were Korean officials fewer in number, then might Li-Hsi know each and all personally; and then might his servants, civil and military, be less complete nonentities on the one hand, and more invariably worthy on the other, in the great pageant of Asia's Western civilization-ship.

The Chinese call their Emperor "The Son of Heaven." The Japanese used to regard their Mikado with as much veneration, and even now speak of him with no less reverence. The Koreans seem to have caught, from China or Japan, the convenient idea of mediation. According to the religious law of Korea, which is seldom marked, and less often respected, only the king is fit to worship the gods. The subjects of the king must content themselves with worshipping him. To venture to pray to the king is as near heaven as an orthodox Korean may dare to come. And the king, if he be in gracious mood, will pass the prayer on to the god who is no more above him than he is above his people.

It seems a Jacob's ladder sort of religion—the religion to which the Koreans pretend (for, as a matter of fact, as I shall try to prove later, they have no religion at all). The peasant throws his paper prayer at the feet of his king; the king, if to him it so seems fit, throws that paper prayer at the feet of the god; and perhaps none of the kingly prerogatives more clearly define the high position of the king than the fact that of all Koreans, he alone is fit to speak to the Korean god.

The royal house of Korea emphatically believes that it is descended from divine and royal spirits. If Li-Hsi cannot prove his descent from the denizens of the Korean heaven, we certainly cannot disprove it; and he has the courage of his convictions, for neither he nor any prince of his blood will wed with a maiden who cannot claim as exceptional, as divine, and as ethereal an ancestry. This keeps the royal family of Korea almost as narrowly blooded as the royal family of Siam.

Tinsel has not yet gone off the market even in Europe. Newsboys and Eton boys jostle each other on the curb-stones of Northumberland Avenue in their boyish desire to see a modern Lord Mayor's Show. In the Orient tinsel is almost as common a commodity, as necessary an adjunct of daily life as is rice itself. When the King of Korea goes forth from his palace grounds he is followed by, preceded by, a glittering throng. Nobles, soldiers, secretaries, and servants arrayed in barbaric splendour, and carrying a hundred symbols of Asiatic majesty, attend upon him; and over him is carried a canopy rich with gold and jewels. Music, unless the king forbid, sounds his approach. But no other sound is heard. No one may speak. The procession moves slowly, silently. The very horses step softly, and would sooner think of cantering backwards than of neighing. The horsemen are followed by footmen. Both carry banners and insignia.

Immediately before the king walks a secretary of state. He carries an elaborate box. I have heard Koreans speak of it as "the mercy-box." The king's ear is open to the meanest of his subjects, in theory at least. When the king goes forth his route is probably strewn with papers, papers are thrown from over walls, papers hang by strings from windows and roofs, sticks are placed along the roadside, and in their notched or forked ends are more papers. All these papers are scrupulously gathered up and put into the " mercy-box." Each paper contains a petition or the story of a wrong for which the sufferer beseeches the king's redress. These papers are opened by the king in person, after he has returned to the palace. He and he alone decides which of the petitions shall be granted and how; which shall be refused. Often only he ever knows by whom they have been written.

Such is the outing of a Korean king, or rather such it was until a very few years ago. Within six or seven years the ceremonial has been slightly altered. Until then it had remained almost unchanged for centuries. Whether Li-Hsi will ever again go forth in like state I question. It's more likely that, if he lives and reigns, he will be sending to London or Calcutta for a brougham. But of this I feel sure: while he continues to sit in power upon Korea's throne, his ears will be keen to hear the cries of his people, and his heart hot to serve them.

CHAPTER V.

It has been very often said that the position of woman is more deplorable in Korea than in any other civilized or semi-civilized country. And I have comparatively little to urge against the statement. Certainly woman's life seems narrower in Korea than in either China or Japan, or in Burmah, or Siam, or in India. Socially and politically, in Korea, woman simply does not exist. She has not even a name. After marriage she is called by her husband's name with the prefix of Mrs. Before marriage she has not even this pretence to a name. There is one exception, and, I think, one only to this rule. The geisha girls have names of their own, but then the geisha girls have individuality; live lives, if not moral, why still, not colourless, and mix with men, if not on an equality, at least with a good deal of familiarity; and it would be rather awkward if the men who are dependent upon them for female society in anything approaching a Western sense, had no name by which to call them. The "Fragrant Iris" was the name of a geisha girl whose acquaintance Mr. Lowell tells us he made in Korea, and four of her companions were called "Peach Blossom," "Plum Flower," "Rose," and "Moonbeam."

Korean girls, long before they reach a marriageable age, live in the seclusion of the women's quarters. After her betrothal a girl belongs not to her father but to her mother-in-law. Upon marriage she becomes the property of her husband, and is, in most cases, immediately taken to his dwelling. As in China, married sons live with their fathers. Sometimes three or four generations of one family occupy one home. But, unlike Chinese wives, each Korean wife has a room or rooms of her own. The only man who (in most families) ever enters them is her husband. Unlike the wives of China, she may not, as a rule, be visited by her husband's father, her husband's brother, or her husband's grandfather. But should his father or his grandfather fall ill, it is not only her privilege, but her duty, to leave the women's quarters, and, going to his bedside, nurse him until he dies or recovers.

There are one or two advantages in being a woman in Korea. There are very few crimes for

which a Korean woman can be punished. Her
husband is answerable for her conduct, and must
suffer in her stead if she breaks any ordinary
law.

Korean women are not uneducated, though they
never go to schools; and books and materials
for writing and painting are freely at their disposal.

The dress of Korean women is very much more
like the dress of European women than is that
of the women of almost any other Oriental race.
They wear petticoats made very much in Western
fashion, but stiffly starched into crinoline-like un-
gracefulness. The women of the poorer classes
wear these skirts above their ankles. The
women of wealth or of rank wear skirts touching
the ground. They wear a jacket or belt shaped
very much like, and answering the purpose of, a
corset, and a shorter jacket which is at best but
an inadequate neckerchief. And under their
petticoat they wear three pairs of wide trousers.
Except among the very poorest class, respectable
Korean women muffle themselves in a garment
like a dress or great-coat whenever they go
abroad. Boys and girls are dressed alike until
they are five years old.

Among the poor all the household work is done
by women, but among the rich the women have

no domestic duties except those of nursing and sewing. All the garments of a Korean family are made by the women of the family. The purchase of a ready-made garment, or to hire it made, would be considered a disgrace to the family, and a deeper disgrace to its women. Korean ladies sew as exquisitely as French nuns, and embroider as deftly as those Japanese men whose profession embroidery is.

Korean girls are usually married between the ages of seventeen and twenty-two; and if married to a bachelor, he is almost invariably three or five, and often even eight, years their junior. But when a widower marries, or a man takes a second, or third, or fourth wife, he invariably selects a woman younger than himself.

Among the mandarin classes polygamy is a duty, and every mandarin is expected to keep at least several concubines or second-class wives in his yamun.

In Söul, and in one other large city, children are commonly betrothed when the boy is seven or eight, but it is not so in the other parts of Korea. Korean widows must remain unmarried, or marry men who are the social inferiors of their dead husbands. And in Korea, as in China, a widow who re-marries is disgraced, and becomes more or less of a social outcast.

The customs preliminary to marriage are in Korea very like those same customs in China and in Japan. The father of a marriageable daughter or a marriageable son looks about for a suitable *parti*. If a husband is desired, then the girl's father usually interviews a number of eligible youths, widowers, or married men until he finds what he wants. Then a middle-man is sent to discover whether an offer of marriage would be favourably received, and on what terms. If the bridegroom selected is unmarried he has, unless he is an orphan and the head of his family, no voice whatever in the matter, the only people really consulted being the respective fathers. If a father is on the look-out for a daughter-in-law, he sends his wife to interview and report upon the girl whom he has been told is suitable in age, dower, etc. Now comes in another of the few advantages of being a woman in Korea. She has very largely the selection of her own daughters-in-law, and if the daughter-in-law proves unsatisfactory she has only herself to blame. When the middle-man has ascertained that the proposal of marriage will be acceptable, the father who has negotiated the proceedings writes an elaborate letter to the other father, and makes a formal proposal for the hand of his son or daughter. But this letter is not binding upon the writer until he receives one in return accepting the proposal.

After that there is no drawing back, and should the betrothed man die before the marriage day the girl is regarded as a widow, and must remain unmarried all her life, or else marry an inferior and with disgrace. The man, on the other hand—should she die—is entirely free to marry, and at once.

When a lucky day has been selected for the wedding, the bridegroom sends to the bride presents in the Japanese fashion. Female clothing, bits of stuff, and sweets are the most important items among these presents. When they have been sent and received, the marriage ceremony has been half performed. Then the bridegroom is allowed to knot up his hair in manly fashion, but not until the day of marriage is he allowed to assume the garb of a man—be dressed as a man. A Korean bachelor of seventy is regarded as a child, treated as a child, and dressed as a child.

A prospective bridegroom pays visits of respect not to the relations of his bride, but to the kinsfolk of his own father. The kinsfolk of his mother do not count; indeed, a Korean wife is supposed to have no kindred but the kindred of her husband. The bridegroom's father gives a great feast upon the night of the day on which the presents are sent. The feast lasts all night, and the quantity of food eaten, and the quantity of wine drunk, would sound almost incredible to European ears.

Korea is the country of bachelors. There are two reasons for this. The majority of the people are very poor and cannot afford the expense of daughters-in-law. Then, too, polygamy is so extensively practised among the rich that the supply of girls in the marriage market is never equal to the demand, and the average Korean would far rather see his daughter become the second, or the seventh, or the eighth wife, or concubine of a rich or powerful man, than the one wife of a labourer or low-class man. Marriage usually takes place three days after the presents are sent. These three days are very busy ones to the Korean bride, for out of one of the pieces of stuff sent her by the bridegroom, she must herself, and without assistance, fashion the elaborate robe which he assumes on the marriage night, and which is his first garment made after adult fashion. Thus the three days before marriage are spent by a Korean girl in performing her first duty as a wife. And the sending of the garment signifies that she, with the assistance of whatever wives he may afterwards marry, will, so long as they both live, make all the clothing required by him, his children, and his women.

When the marriage day arrives the lucky hour is chosen, and the bridegroom departs for the house of the bride. The bridegroom's procession is as long and as splendid as his purse, or the purse of his father, can possibly permit. Everyone in that procession rides on horseback, and in single file. First comes a servant-man on a horse richly caparisoned; this servant carries a life-sized image of a wild goose. It is covered by a red scarf, and the servant must hold it with both hands—a circumstance which makes his horseback riding interesting, if not perilous. After him comes the bridegroom, splendidly arrayed, and followed by a groom and all his other servants. After them rides the bridegroom's father, and he, too, is followed by all the servants he possesses or has been able to borrow. Relatives and friends in great quantity of persons and great quality of garments bring up the splendid rear.

In a marriage procession, or at a marriage, the poorest and lowliest man in Korea is allowed to wear robes and hats as rich as those ordinarily worn by the highest dignitary in the land, if he can manage to get them, and of the same distinctive style and shape.

When the girl's house is reached, the servant

who has carried the goose dismounts, the others remain on horseback. He goes into the house and lays the goose upon a bowl of rice that is standing in a convenient place. Then, without speaking, he leaves the house. The bridegroom's father dismounts next, then the bridegroom, then all the others. Before entering the house they take off their boots and their hats, and their outer robes. The bride's father now comes out of his house, bids them welcome, and leads them in. He is immediately followed by the bridegroom, and then by the bridegroom's father and the others. They all sit solemnly down, and then ensues a scene not to be beaten for noise, no, not even in all Asia, which, I assure you, is saying a good deal.

The bridegroom has been accompanied, as far as practicable, by all the youths or men who are, or were, his fellow-students, or who belonged to the same literary degree as himself. These seize upon him with shrieking, and laughter, and singing, carrying him off to some distant part of the house or compound, and refuse, under any circumstances, to give him up, or to allow the marriage to proceed. The girl's father, after some time, offers them a present of money to depart, and leave the chief actor in the proposed function free to play his part. After a good deal of haggling, and when the bribe has reached as high a point as the rollickers think it probably will, they accept the money and depart with it, to spend it in a day and a night of roystering and banqueting.

A feast elaborate, and to European notions tedious, is then offered to the bridegroom, his father and their attendants. After the feast the bridegroom's father and all the servants depart. The bride's father leads the bridegroom to the room in which the ancestral tablets of the family are enshrined; for ancestral worship is as universal and as sincere in Korea as in China. Before these tablets the prospective husband must pay homage long and earnest.

Late in the evening the bridegroom is taken into the room of the bride, whom he has not as yet seen. The room is empty, and he is immediately left there alone; but the room is fragrant with iris, or sweet with great bowls and branches of cherry-blossom, and splendid with wisteria or magnificent bunches of the Korean peony. Two great bowls are there heaped with rice, and in the centre of each bowl stands a brilliantly yellow candlestick, holding a taper that is perfumed and lit. After a time, the bride comes into the room, led by her mother, and surrounded by all her kinswomen. No one speaks; the mother and the relatives go out, as soon as they have fairly come in. The door is closed, and the bride lifts her veil. On the following day, the young wife divides into two the hair which hitherto hung down her back in one long plait. She twists one part of it on to the left side of her head, and one on to the right, and so she wears her hair for the rest of her life, taking it down only to dress it or have it dressed, or to dishevel it about her shoulders as a sign of mourning, on the death of her husband, or one of his relatives. On the third day after the marriage the young couple repair to the house of the bridegroom or the bridegroom's father. They may, however, elect to remain a little longer in the home of the bride's people, but unless they leave on the third day they are compelled to remain where they are for an entire year.

Thirty years before Christ it was customary for a bridegroom to dwell under the roof of his father-in-law until the first son had been born, and attained to years of manhood. This is still the custom in some parts of Korea, and among some Korean families. Whether the husband and wife go to the home of his family three days, one year, or many years after marriage, they must, upon entering the door, at once go to the tablets of his ancestors, bend before them innumerable times, and repeat to them innumerable prayers and benedictions.

Korean marriage certificates are rather quaint. They are on red paper, of course, for red is the colour of happiness, and is used throughout China and Korea for the records of births, marriages, for calling cards, and all such things. These marriage certificates are inscribed with the usual Chinese characters, but what makes them peculiarly interesting is the fact that during the marriage ceremony they are equally divided, one half is given to the husband, and one to the wife. It is the only instance I know of a country in which it is thought necessary to provide the bridegroom with a certificate of the marriage. But in Korea marriage is even of more importance to men than to women. Marriage makes all the difference possible in the life of a Korean man—it does not alter so very much the life of a Korean woman. He passes from boyhood to manhood in the twinkling of an eye; he takes precedence of all bachelors whatever their age; can insult them or jostle them in the streets with perfect impunity. Marriage alters the daily life of the woman very little. It opens to her all the possibilities of maternity, and secures her the occasional society of her husband, and, as I have said, it puts up her hair. But I can think of no other material way in which it affects her. She passes from one Korean house to another Korean house, and the two are probably identical in their interior arrangements, furnishings, and decorations, at least, so far as the women's premises are concerned. She eats the same food that she ate with her own mother and sisters. She reads the same books, does the same needlework. If her husband be poor, she performs the same drudgery. She hears the same talk, thinks the same thoughts, and has, or lacks, the same amusements that she has all her life. To be sure she sees about her the faces of, for a time, strange women, but their lives and their minds are so similar to those of the women she has always lived with, that their companionship cannot possibly make any violent difference in her or in her existence.

There is one very important reason why his half of the marriage certificate should be, and is, zealously preserved by the husband : without it he cannot procure another wife should his first die, or be divorced, or prove inadequate. Her half of the brilliant paper is no such talisman to the wife. Divorced, she can never re-marry ; widowed, she can only re-wed with degradation.

The marriage ceremony differs somewhat in different parts of Korea, among different classes of people, and among different families. Often the noisy students take no part in the function, and the bride is present at the marriage feast. The bride in this case remains veiled, eats nothing and says nothing, until the repast is over. Indeed, in many parts of Korea the bride must not speak during her wedding day. At the end of the feast the bride and groom bow to each other three times, and then the bride throws back her veil, and they are man and wife.

In an antique paper or essay on the moral and domestic condition of Korea, a paper written by one of the old French missionaries who penetrated into Korea long before European commerce, or European politics, had dared to do so, or at least, succeeded in doing so, I found a description of a wedding ceremony differing somewhat from either of the above. And yet so the marriage ceremony often is even to-day in parts of Korea. The translation is very free :—

'On the nuptial day both bride and groom cease to wear their hair as children wear it. Her hair is arranged by some maiden of her kindred—his arranged by some bachelor of his blood. These two amateur hair-dressers are called "hands of honour," and after the bride and groom, and their respective fathers, are the most important personages at a Korean marriage.

'The bridegroom, accompanied by all his male relatives and all his male friends, on the morning of the marriage day, goes to the bride's house.

There she is given to him, and he carries her off to his house, or to the house of his father. In the best room of that house a platform or marriage altar has been arranged. It is very rich with embroidered cloths, carved pieces, vessels of metal, jewelled ornaments, and as many of the wonderful Korean flowers as are in season. Platters of rice and fruits, and of sweetmeats and nuts, are usually there too, and incense-sticks ; and candles must by no means be absent. The bride and the bridegroom step up on to the platform from opposite sides ; both are elaborately dressed, perfumed, and be-jewelled, and the bride is heavily painted. She wears a veil and innumerable odd ornaments at her throat, about her neck, at her girdle, on her breast, and on her back. The bridegroom wears a marriage hat, for in this strange peninsula, not only every rank, and every age, and every season, but almost every event calls for a hat of special shape and material. The couple bow to each other profoundly a number of times, and then leave the platform—she going to the home of her new seclusion, the women's quarters of her husband's house, and he going to his own rooms or to those of his father. All the women present follow her ; all the men follow him. For a week or longer, if the father of the groom or the groom be a man of wealth, a great feast is held both in the women's quarters and in the reception rooms of the men. Often the guests remain throughout this period, or if they go home occasionally to sleep, they are sure to return in a very few hours for more to eat, and more to drink. During the ceremony, and during the week of rejoicing, the bridesmaids are busy filling "the cup of mutual joy" with nuptial wine. From this cup the bride and the bridegroom drink together during the ceremony, but afterwards it is sent from the apartments of the one to the apartments of the other, and *vice versâ*. At the marriage feast there must be a goose, a dried pheasant, emblems of braided or twisted straw, arrack, and gourds, and other fruits tied with tinselled and crimson ribbons: for these are the Korean symbols of marital felicity.'

Often the girl of eight who is betrothed to a boy of five, or a girl of twelve who is betrothed to a boy of eight, goes at once to her father-in-law's house, and is then and there lost to her own family. So entirely does a Korean woman become a member of her husband's family, that after marriage she wears mourning for him and his relatives only, and gives no sign of grief at the death of her own relatives, should she chance to be informed of it. During the period of betrothal the bride and bridegroom must each mourn for the death of any of their kindred, and the marriage cannot take place while either of the parties are in mourning. Korean mourning is as long, or longer than Chinese mourning. Parents are mourned for three years or more, and other relatives for shorter, but not short periods. It will be readily seen that a goodly number of deaths in both families delay a marriage far beyond the limits of all human patience, save that which characterizes the Far East. It is not unusual for a marriage to be delayed for ten years in such a way, and betrothed couples have been kept waiting thirty, and even thirty-five years, before one or the other, or both of them, could lay aside the robes of mourning for the brilliant vestments of marriage. This is the reason, I believe the chief reason, why for hundreds of years the population of Korea has not increased. Other reasons are the fearful infant mortality, and the horrible and periodical recurrence of epidemics.

Next to being a woman, perhaps the most unfortunate thing that can happen to anyone in Korea is to be poor. But if there are several advantages in being a woman even there, there is, at least, one in being poor. Among the poor it is often the custom for the bride and bridegroom to meet a month or more before the marriage, and if either of them is dissatisfied they cannot be forced to fulfil the engagement.

Korean wives have one rather desirable prerogative—a prerogative which the wives of China do not share with them, nor I fancy, do the wives of Japan. A Korean man cannot house his concubines or second-class wives under the roof that shelters his true or first wife, without her permission. Strangely enough, the first wife very rarely objects to living in rather close companionship with the other women of her husband's household. Perhaps the longing for human companionship is stronger than jealousy in woman's breast. And perhaps it is because the companionship of men is forbidden her, that a Korean wife comes to not only tolerate, but to enjoy the companionship of the women who share with her her husband's affection, attention, and support.

Korean women have not always lived in the strict seclusion in which they live now. Some of the older historians, Chinese and others, describe the appearance of the women and their manners without any hint that seeing them and knowing of them was anything unusual. And Hamel boasts that his blonde beard and that of his fellows, and their blue eyes, found great favour with the women of Quelpaert. In the days of Hamel, as now, the inhabitants of Quelpaert were purely Korean. Almost ever since Korea obtained Quelpaert from Japan, the island has been used as a sort of penal settlement; a place of confinement for foreigners who are unfortunate or unwise enough to land upon the shores of the peninsula, and for grave Korean miscreants who escape the death penalty. But it has also had always a goodly number of inhabitants, of the freemen and the official classes, and all of these, as well as the great bulk of prisoners, have been unmixedly Korean. And the freedom and publicity enjoyed by the women of the island, in Hamel's time, was doubtless also enjoyed by the women of the peninsula. On the other hand, Hamel may have written only of the women of the labouring class. But even so his testimony—and when has Hamel been proved untruthful?—proves that during the last two hundred years times have greatly changed for Korean women. To-day no Korean woman, however lowly, would look up at a strange man long enough to like him; much less "look to like, if looking liking move."

In every Korean house of any pretension the women's apartments are in the most secluded part of the building. They open on to a garden, and never on to a street. The compound is walled, and no two families ever live upon the same compound. And no Korean may go upon the roof of his own house without legal permission, and without giving due notice to all his neighbours. The roof may leak, and the roof may crack in the middle, but before the owner of the house or any mechanic in his employ may go up to see what the matter is, and to remedy it, the occupiers of every house, the garden of which can be seen from his roof, must be notified, and ample time given for the ladies of those various establishments to leave the gardens. So a Korean woman is as hidden from the world, in her husband's garden or summer-house, as is a nun in her cell.

The wives and daughters of well-to-do Koreans spend a great deal of time in their gardens, sharing naturally enough the intense love of their menkind for nature, and probably finding their peculiar lives more endurable among the trees and the birds and the lotus ponds, than they do in their queer little rooms, through the paper windows of which they cannot look unless they poke a hole with their fingers first—rooms in which there is little space and less furniture.

After the curfew rings it is illegal for a Korean man to leave his own house, unless under circumstances which I have stated in a previous chapter; then it becomes legal for Korean women to slip out and take the air and gossip freely. But both the law and the privilege have fallen somewhat into abeyance, especially in Söul. There are now so many foreigners in Söul, members of legations, and servants connected with legations, that it has been found impossible to keep the streets of Söul free from men after curfew, and so the women of Söul have very greatly lost that which was, a few years ago, one of their few, and one of their most dearly prized privileges.

If the *dramatis personæ* in Korean society are all men, not so the *dramatis personæ* in Korea's history. As in China, and as in Japan, important parts have been played by women in the great historical drama of Korea—a drama that began centuries and centuries ago, and that is not ended yet, or only now ending. Korea has had many remarkable women who have left their as yet indelible stamp upon the customs and the laws of their country, and upon the thought of their countrymen. Korea has had at least three great queens. Korea has had her Boadicea. The present King of Korea owes his kingship, in large part at least, to his great-grandmother, Dowager Queen Chō, who adopted him, and in 1864 was largely instrumental in securing for him the throne to which the royal consul had elected him.

The most powerful women of whom we can read in the history of India, from the time of the

Rock Temples to the time of the Indian Mutiny,
were purdah-women ; and the woman who has
perhaps had more influence and more power
over her own husband than ever other woman
had over other husband—the woman who was
perhaps at her death the most sincerely mourned,
and the woman who was entombed as no other
woman has ever yet been entombed, and probably
as no other woman will ever be entombed—the
beautiful Arjamand Banu—lived in the strictest
purdah. And until the breaking out of the
Chino-Japanese war, the most powerful person
in Korea was, and for twenty years had been, a
woman, the king's wife. Queen Min, for even
she has no name, and is known only by the name
of the race from which she has sprung, comes of
one of the two great intellectual families of
Korea ; and the great family of Min has produced no cleverer woman or man than the wife
of Li-Hsi.

A very large proportion of the literature at our
disposal, which treats in any dignified way of
Korea, has been written by missionaries. This is
inevitably so of any Asiatic country whose first
Western invaders have been soldiers of the Cross.
Fortunately for the interested student of Korea,
the missionaries who have gone to Korea seem
almost from the first to have been mentally,

socially, and in culture, equipped above the missionary average in other parts of heathendom. Whether they have had a corresponding moral superiority it would be interesting to know, but I am the last person in the world competent to judge the moral status of a missionary. This of the European missionaries in Korea—from the Jesuit fathers old France sent there to the Presbyterian brethren recently sent from the United States—a surprising number of them had the gift not of writing (for scribbling seems to come as naturally to the average missionary as to the average nineteenth-century woman), but of writing well, and with great discretion. If we would learn the history of Korea, we must learn it very largely from the writings of European missionaries, unless, indeed, we are able to read Chinese, and have access to the fuller, more ably written, and probably more authentic histories of Korea, written by Chinese *littérateurs*. It is a matter of course that the Chinese, who are akin to the Koreans, and who may almost be said to have brought them up, should make fewer blunders in writing of Chosön than men of utterly dissimilar race and thought habits. Then, too, the writing of the Chinese histories of Korea has been largely contemporaneous with the enactment of that history. And no man can write with entire breadth of a people to whose religion he is bitterly antagonistic.

One blunder is conspicuous in most of the valuable books written by Europeans—written on Korea. They state almost to a volume that the women are uneducated and never pretty.

Educated after European methods they certainly are not. But why should they be? And that they are not—does that prove that they are not educated at all? There are more systems of education than one.

Let us take the poor women of Söul, and compare them with the poor women of Liverpool or of London, and with the women of many tongues, who flock into New York through the portals of Castle Garden. The Korean women can read and write, the large majority of them. They cook well, cleanly, and economically. Out of a few simple ingredients (which her Western sister would scorn), and with a few simple implements (that that sister would not understand)—often almost without implements and with little fire—fire that must be coaxed and humoured, and humoured and coaxed, the poorest Korean woman will prepare a meal which no hungry European, prince or peasant, need scorn to eat. It will be savoury, wholesome, clean to daintiness, and pleasantly served. They can sew, make all that they, their husbands, and their children wear, can these poor, ignorant, heathen women. They are expert washerwomen. Most of them can make pictures with sharp sticks, or with brush, and almost all of them are more or less skilled in midwifery, in the care of the sick, in sick-room cookery, and in the care of children. They know how to keep their tempers, hold their tongues, control their appetites, to make much of little, and to enjoy to the full and with thanksgiving any small pleasure that falls to their scantily pleasured lot. Now let us turn to the Seven Dials, or to the Five Points—No, on second thought let us not!

As for Korean gentlewomen, they are skilled in Korean music, in Chinese and Korean literature. They are unsurpassed mistresses of the needle, more than able with the brush, and thoroughly acquainted with every detail of the complicated Korean etiquette. They are deft in the nice ceremonies of the toilet. They know the histories of Korea, of China, and perhaps of Japan. They are familiar with their own folk-lore, and can repeat it glibly and picturesquely. They are nurses and mothers and wives by nature, and wives, mothers, nurses, and accoucheuses by training. Above all, they are taught (and they learn) to be amiable. They are instructed in the art of charming, and in the grace of being gentle, as soon as they are taught to walk. I have known advanced women in Europe who could scarcely boast of being more highly educated. And the happiest women I have known have not always been the most learned. I think that we are apt to underrate the education of women in the East because it differs so essentially from ours : but then so do their physique and the country in which they live ; its flora, its climate, and its sociology. A Korean once told me (he was a kinsman of Queen Min, a traveller, a linguist, and a man of—cosmopolitanly speaking—most considerable attainments) that his wife was more widely and more throughly versed in Chinese literature, modern and classic, than he. And Chinese literature is indisputably the greatest literature that Asia has ever produced.

The Queen of Korea is, with the possible exception of the Dowager Empress of China, as well educated as any royal lady in Asia.

As to the national lack of beauty among the women of Korea—why, it is neither more nor less than nonsense, ignorant, and rather stupid nonsense. I know no race in which the women who earn their individual slice, and a goodly share of the family loaf, in the sweat of their brows retain their beauty long. The women seen on the streets of Söul and in the fields, and on the mountain slopes of Korea, belong—if I may for the sake of emphasis repeat myself—belong to the hardest-worked, the most weather-beaten, burden-bent, and ill-fed class in Korea. Their personal appearance is no indication of the real type of Korean womanhood. They are painted by the sun and the wind, disfigured with trouble and back-ache, and their once pretty faces have been profaned by many tears, and they are hideous. But the women of the Korean leisure class are, as a rule (a rule with only just enough exceptions to prove it), undeniably pretty—pretty with a prettiness that is closely akin to the prettiness of the women of Japan and Burmah. The Queen of Korea is quaintly pretty, and among the three hundred women who are, nominally at least, the concubines of the king, and among the very many female attendants of their two Majesties, there is scarcely a plain face. Of course many Europeans who have been resident in Korea, and have written of their residence, have not had access to the court, much less to the Queen and her ladies. But surely any wide-eyed man who has spent some time in Korea has seen and seen again the geisha girls. Who that has lived in Korea denies their beauty? And would it not occur to an observer of somewhat less than abnormal reasoning power that since the only female members he had ever seen of the Korean leisure class were beautiful, that it was fairly presumable that the Korean women who worked even less, and lived in greater luxury, and under more healthy conditions, were at least as beautiful?

Korean women (those of them who have not been scarred by over-toil, nor deformed by privation) have remarkably small, and remarkably pretty hands and feet, and of nothing are they prouder than of their dimpled fingers, and their shapely, delicate feet. But the feet of a Korean woman are small by nature, never by art. They have lovely eyes—these women—musical voices, and are graceful of motion.

The Queen is pale and delicate-looking. She has a remarkable forehead, low but strong, and a mouth charming in its colouring, in its outlines, in its femininity, in the pearls it discloses, and sweet with the music that slips through it when she speaks. She dresses plainly as a rule, and in dark but rich materials. In this she resembles the high-born matrons of Japan. And in cut her garments are more Japanese than those of other Korean women: she wears her hair parted in the middle, and drawn softly into a simple knot or coil of braid. She wears diamonds most often; not many, but of much price. They are her favourite gems. In this one particular she is almost alone among the women of the East; for pearls are the beloved jewels of almost every woman and girl-child that is born in the Orient.

Queen Min has been as assiduous as she has been powerful in advancing the interests of her family—the family of her birth I mean, for her marriage—unlike the marriages of other Korean women—has no whit divorced her from the people of her blood. All the desirable offices in Korea were held for years by her kinsmen.

Queen Min has not only been the power behind the Korean throne, but she has been, even more than the King, the all-seeing eye of Korea. Her spies have been everywhere, seen everything, reported everything.

Two things that are true of the Queen are peculiarly significant of the grip that Oriental customs have upon the most autocratic of Oriental minds. She—the most powerful Korean in Korea —is content to be nameless; a sovereign with almost unlimited power, but without a nominal individuality; and to be called merely by the family name of her forefathers, and to be designated only as the daughter of her fathers, the wife of her husband, and the mother of her son.

It strikes an Occidental as even more strange that a woman so supremely powerful with her husband and king should be so graciously tolerant of the women of his harem. She not only tolerates them, she seems to like them, to take pride in them, and she is on the friendliest terms with Li-Hsi's eldest son, who is also the son of a concubine. True her own son is the crown prince, but it is probable that his elder brother and not he will be Korea's next king, if the present dynasty be destined to have another king. Li Hsia—Queen Min's son—is not the imbecile he has been reported, but he has not the greatest mental strength, and less strength of body.

Queen Min is admirable and affable in her home circle. She is a woman of no great physical strength. But she has considerable courage, moral and physical, and both have been well tried.

Queen Min has always advocated the opening of Korea to foreigners, and the establishing of relations with foreign Powers. Whether this shows her wisdom or her folly it is too soon to say: but it certainly proves her—woman of the Far East that she is—to have a mind of her own, even though she lacks a personal name.

No one man or woman who wishes to have a part in the solving of the great and complicated woman-question should fail to make an, as far as possible, exhaustive study of the women of Asia. The women of the East differ from the women of the West, chiefly in being more secluded from public places, public duties, and public influence; in being more confined to, and more absorbed in their own firesides; in being less on a nominal equality with man, and in being more definitely, if less happily and less highly placed in the State and in the family. They differ from the women of the West in the manner of their education, and in the aims of their education.

Before we consider whether these differences are to the advantage or disadvantage of Eastern women, it is only fair that we (we Western women who are interested in working out, not only our own salvation, but the salvation of mankind) should consider very carefully how the position of woman in the East has affected man in the East, and the Eastern races in their entireties. Does the absence of woman from the general daily life of a race render that daily life less refined, and more brutal? One might, at first thought, have concluded so. We may assume for a premise that women are more refined, more gentle of heart, and more graceful of manner than men, and it is, I believe, commonly thought among the great mass of people in the West, who are almost altogether uninformed and altogether ill-informed about the East, that the men of the East are brawlers, half-savage, and uncouth. No grosser mistake could be made. Probably the two most brutalizing passions are envy and jealousy. There have been in the history of the world, I think, no two other causes of so much bloodshed, so much brutality, so much infinite cruelty, and so much horrible vulgarity. The wrangling over women, the rivalry for women, and the suspicions and the enormous heartburns occasioned by these rivalries have, in the lands where the women mingled freely with the men, more than counterbalanced the refining effect produced by the fact that the men of these countries have wished to appear at their best before the women, and have been on the whole inspired to civility and gentle behaviour in the presence of women. Because an Oriental's wife is his property, unquestionably so, she is the cause of no bloodshed, no jealousy, and her refining influence is more proved in the breach than in the observance. The Korean gentleman, the Chinese mandarin, or the husband of a high-caste Hindoo woman who goes to a dinner-party, has the soothing consciousness that his wife is safe at home. Under lock and key, perhaps : certainly debarred, by the strong prejudices of centuries, from going abroad, or showing her face to men. He can devote himself with placid heart and undiverted mind to the meat and drink set before him and the men sitting about him. No

torturing wonder as to which of his wife's platonic
friends has dropped in to have an after-dinner
cup of coffee with her can come to destroy his
appreciation of the fine flavour of his soup. He
can glance around that dinner table with eyes
fearless and proud, for they will not encounter his
wife flirting, ever so harmlessly, with someone
else's husband : a sight calculated to make any
man whose heart is not made of dough, and his
brain of pulp, choke over his cutlets, and end his
dinner miserably in a fit of ill-humour and indiges-
tion. True, on the other hand, he is not able
to flirt with his neighbour's wife. The social
arrangements are such, in the East, that no fairly
well-to-do man need lack ample female society
both at home and abroad. But the female society
which is open to him outside of his own house is
not the society of wives, mothers, nor of maidens.
And moreover, the majority of men enjoy a good
stag-dinner very much more than they do an
equally good feast which is shared with them by
a number of women. When a party of gentlemen
dine together, in the East, or in the West, I very
much fear that their table-talk is far more intellectual, entertaining, and altogether worth while
than the table-talk of women who dine with each
other, or of men and women who dine together.
And I am sure that it is quite as refined, free from

undesirable insinuations, coarse witticisms, and imbecile pleasantries. I am not speaking, of course, of dinners *tête-à-tête*, nor would anything I have said apply to them. I have been an unseen spectator of many stag-dinners in the East, and I was once an unseen, but all-seeing, guest at a stag-dinner in the West. And in my salad days I have often broken bread with women, women, only women. It is my conclusion that the European men who dine at their clubs, and the Asiatic men who dine with their fellows, gain almost as much as they lose, and I can partly understand man's preference for the table companionship of men. I believe that good digestion waits on appetite more often in dinner parties of the East than in dinner parties of the Occident.

The Eastern man rarely or never commits the sin of coveting his neighbour's wife, because he rarely or never sees her, and so, at least, we cannot say that the unrighteous laws governing the relative positions of the sexes in the Orient, lead the men of the Orient into the worst of all temptations. Among the very poorest classes in Korea the men invariably see more or less of the women; but those men are too poor, too hard worked, too absorbed, body, brain, and heart, in a struggle for existence to covet other men's wives, or, often indeed, to have wives of their own.

Oriental polygamy seems so delicate a subject, such thin conversational ice to the average Western mind, that the best informed writers are rather in the habit of skating about its edges and of speaking loosely and indefinitely, and with the greatest confusion about the wives and the concubines of the East. I have spoken of the well-to-do Korean as having a plurality of wives. This is not so. And that such a mis-statement has been made by writers of eminence, and ordinarily of great exactness, is no excuse for me. A Korean can have but one wife, one true and absolute wife, but (and here comes in the fact which is hard, very hard, of comprehension even to intelligent Europeans, who have not lived in the Orient) he may have as many concubines as he can afford, and their position, though not so high of rank, is as honourable, and as respectable as that of his wife. The word concubine, in the sense given it by our English dictionaries, can no more justly be applied to the women of a Korean's seraglio than it can be applied to Hagar. I use the word, because it is the word used by all European scholars to indicate the women of whom I am writing, and is also the word used to designate them in the countries of the East. As I have said, they are not on a social equality with the wife, but they are, to the best of my belief, on a moral equality with her, both in the eyes of Oriental law and in the eyes of morality itself. I see no difference ethically between the woman who consents to marry (as every well-born Korean woman does consent to marry) a man who she knows has, or will have, a well filled harem—I see no difference between her and the woman who consents to make that harem her home.

A Korean's concubines are almost as absolutely the handmaidens of his wife as of himself. They must serve her and do her bidding, and can only escape from this in the rare instance when one rises in the man's eyes to higher favour than the wife.

The children of a concubine do not as a rule rank with the children of a wife, but they are neither despised nor shamed. They are born to a slightly lower rank, it is true, but that signifies little, for in Korea every man must carve out his own niche in the social rock, and they, the children of the handmaidens, have as fair a start in life, and as clean a name, as the children of the wife. In this, at least, Korean civilization puts us to the blush.

I am not advocating polygamy. It seems to me an evil only less than the evil which makes innocent children nameless, and unfortunate women homeless and hopeless. It is an evil, I am convinced, that can never work in the West, never be endured by the women of the West. But it does work in the East—works fairly well. And I think it just possible that with the Orientals, with their quickly developed bodies, and their slowly developed minds, it is, under existing circumstances, the lesser of two evils, one of which would be inevitable. In Utah I have known a great many Mormons. I knew Brigham Young when I was a child, and I have since known several of his wives, and many of his children. With the exception of Brigham Young himself and one woman, who was, in the most brazen sense of the word, an adventuress, I have never known a Mormon of even average intellect. Yet, even so, I never knew the wives of a Mormon man to live in peace together. The men were degraded and brainless; the women degraded, almost imbecile and discontented. But it is not so in the Orient; high caste or high class men are refined, gentlemanly, clean of person, and keen of intellect, and the women in their lesser and feminine way are very fit mates of those men. The women of a Korean household are, as an almost invariable rule, happy together. There is less differentiation between the personalities of an Eastern race than between those of a Western, and this is especially true of the women, I think. The wife and all the concubines of a Korean have tastes in common, habits in common, likes and dislikes and accomplishments in common. It is a matter of course to them to live under the same roof, and at the disposal of the same man, and it never occurs to them to question either its fitness or its desirability. All must yield unquestioning obedience to the husband, and, in his absence, all the concubines must yield and do yield as implicit obedience to the wife. She in return is very apt to make them her playfellows and her bosom friends. The Sarahs of the East are far more just, far more kind to the Hagars of the East than Sarah of old was to the mother of Ishmael. Would that the women of the West, who are secure in their sole wifehood—secure at least in the sole legality of their position, had more humanity for the less fortunately placed women of the West. Whatever the social conditions of the West, the women of the West are, in part at least, responsible for them ; not the outcast women, not the women who have made a public failure of life, but the women of assured positions, of intellect, and of moral weight. Whatever the position of woman is in Korea, however low the standard of morality in Korea, the women of Korea, to-day at least, are in no way responsible for it, in no way—in no direct way at least—able to alter it, and I think it greatly to the credit of Korean wives that they treat with no pharisaical contempt, with no feminine injustice, and with no inhumanity, the women who like themselves are, comparatively speaking, moral and social puppets in the hands of a social system in the regulating of which they have no direct voice.

I think I have said repeatedly, and I am going to again say in a succeeding chapter, that Korea has no religion. Whether the facts I shall be able to give will prove my statement to the majority of readers, I am not quite prepared to say. At all events, there is certainly no civilized country, not excepting China, in which religion counts for so little, and in which the professors of religion are under so positive a social ban as they are in Korea. Yet, strangely enough, in Korea there are not only monks and monasteries, but nuns and nunneries. Both monasteries and nunneries seem to have existed almost as long as Korea has existed in anything like its present social condition. Hamel speaks of two nunneries in Söul, and says that the nuns in one were exclusively women of high birth; that the nuns in the other were maids born of the common people. Their hair was shorn as was the hair of monks, and they performed the same duties, obeyed the same rules as did the monks. There were then, and have been since, a number of other nunneries scattered throughout Korea. But it is certainly several hundred years since any body of nuns defended their house from an invading army, or took any part in Korean warfare, local or otherwise, and I very much doubt if they ever did so. But it is probable that in every other way their lives resembled, as indeed they now resemble, the lives of the religious men. In the days of Hamel the nunneries were maintained by the bounty of the king and some of his principal subjects. The king who was reigning in Korea a little over two hundred years ago (the same of whom Hamel speaks), gave the nuns of Söul permission to marry. There are now no nunneries in Söul, but there are still several in Korea. Besides the nun who is shaven and shorn, there is a female *devotée* called Po-sal, who does not cut her hair, and whose vows are less binding than those of other nuns.

I merely mention the fact that there are nuns in Korea, while on the subject of Korean women, because it is a curious item of what I have been able to learn about the women of Chosön, and is uniquely in contrast to almost all the other items that I have been able to gather.

And now almost last, a few words more about the dress of Chosön's women-folk. As I have said, it is less Oriental-looking than the dress of the women of any other Eastern race, and this is remarkable, if not surprising, because the women of Korea to-day dress exactly as the women of China dressed before the present Chinese dynasty came into power, and the race from which it sprang conquered China. In dress, at least, indeed in many other ways, the Koreans have strictly maintained the habits and the fashions that they adopted from, or that were forced upon them by old China. This is why the men wear no queues and the women do not pinch their feet. In dress and in toilet habits the Koreans of to-day are probably an exact replica of the inhabitants of China, before China became dominated by the Tartars.

The women of Korea's poor almost invariably wear the same colour as do the men of the same class: a blue so pale, so indefinite, and, from a short distance, so imperceptible, that it has generally been called white. Even so exact an observer and so careful a chronicler as Mr. Curzon speaks of " the white-clad Koreans." Mr. Curzon may, by-the-bye, have made several mistakes in writing of the East; but, with the best intentions in the world, I have not been able to discover another of his making. One may differ occasionally from his opinions; one may not always share his likes or his dislikes ; but I assure the student of things Eastern that he can depend absolutely upon the truth of Mr. Curzon's statements of facts, and their exactness.

Korean women of position wear almost every conceivable colour. In China, pink and green are set aside for women, and are sacred to their wearing. I do not think that the women of Korea have the sole right to wear any colour, but they certainly have the right to wear, and the habit of wearing, almost every conceivable colour. Purples and greens are their high favourites, and green is almost invariably the hue—and a bright, deep green at that—of the generously-sleeved dress which the middle-class Korean woman (or on rare occasions, a lady) throws about her head and shoulders when she walks abroad. This green dress, which is used as a cloak, is almost exclusively the garment of the women of the middle class—the women who are not so poor that they are obliged to draw water, or to engage in any other forms of hard labour which would make the covering of their faces impossible—but who, at the same time, are occasionally obliged to go abroad on some matter of household business. Wives and concubines and daughters of mandarins and of men of wealth do not often leave their own (by courtesy) house and gardens. When they do,

they go in palanquins. They enter the palan-
quin in their own court-yard; the blinds or
curtains are tightly closed. The chair is borne
away on the shoulders of coolies, and is usually
followed by one or more female servants or waiting women, who run closely behind it, looking on
the ground, and carrying a fan, which indicates the
rank of the palanquined mistress.

In some parts of Korea, among some classes of
the poor, the women wear a very short white
jacket which barely covers the upper part of the
bosom. This jacket looks like an exaggerated
caricature of the pretty white jacket worn by the
Singalese women.

The dress of a Korean lady is as elaborate as
the dress of a Korean working-woman is plain.
The example of simplicity set by Queen Min is
followed by almost none of the Korean women
who can afford to do otherwise. The wardrobe
of a Korean lady contains garments of silk,
surprising in quantity, and covetable in quality,
but satins are unknown, and the glimmer and
glitter, which is so dear to the eye of every Oriental,
must be made alone by the lustre of silk, and
enhanced by as much tinsel, as many jewels and
ornaments as the wearer can possibly afford.

I have spoken of the brown interspace which is
often seen between the jacket and the skirt of a

Korean woman, but it is only seen among the very poorest, and I believe is a lack of material, and a matter of indifference, rather than an intentional exposure of person. I have never seen a Korean lady—I have never seen a gentle-woman of any Eastern race—*décolleté*, except Japanese ladies in European dress. It seems strange, at first thought, that races, whose standards of sexual morality seem to us so far beneath our own, should be so universally modest in their covering of their persons. I am inclined to think that it is not modesty at all, but rather a peculiar phase of Oriental dignity which causes the people of the East to drape themselves as entirely as possible. Mr. Lowell, whose inimitable book on Korea must be a source of almost endless enjoyment to anyone who has known and delighted in the quaint peninsula, says so exactly what I think we ought to understand about the standpoint from which the Orientals regard dress, and how they have come to so regard it, that I take the liberty of borrowing a page from his volume; one of those books which constantly tempt one to quote them from cover to cover. In discussing the manner in which dress in Eastern Asia has been influenced by woman, Mr. Lowell writes :—

" Her absence has been as potent a force there

as her presence has been elsewhere ; for I think we must admit that to her indirectly is due the following singular feature of Asiatic thought.

" The way in which the far Oriental regards dress is somewhat peculiar. I can think of no simile so descriptive as the connection we tacitly assume between spirit and body. We hardly, in ordinary life, think of the one as devoid of the other, and we regard the latter as at least the sense-impression to us of the person within. So do they with dress. To their eyes it forms an essential part of their conception of the man. Somewhat in like manner we are ourselves impressed by dress, in the customary take-at-what-we-see estimate of our fellows. They differ from us in carrying the real into the ideal.

" This is very strikingly seen in the matter of painting. Perhaps one of the most notable features about far Eastern paintings is its utter ignoring of the human figure. There is a complete void in that branch which among Europeans has always claimed attention—the study of the nude. To them artistically man is nothing but a bundle of habits in the sartorial sense. The practice is not due to an excess of what we call modesty. We may, perhaps, define modesty as the veiling from public gaze of all of ourselves, in person or in mind, except so much as is sanctioned to exposure by conventionality. Substitute 'necessity' for 'conventionality,' and you have the far Eastern definition. Convenience, not convention, is the touchstone of propriety. They have not the smallest objection to being seen in a state of nature where occasion demands it; and, on the other hand, nothing would induce them to exhibit any portion of their persons for the purpose of display. To them to be clothed or naked is a matter of indifference; it is merely a question of temporary comfort. The reason why they disregard the body is other than this. It is simply that they have never been led to regard the body as beautiful. That this is so, is due to the low position of woman. She has never risen high enough in their estimation to attain even to that poor level of admiration—that of being an object of beauty. All that should be her birthright they heap as a dowry upon Nature.

"The study of drapery has benefited at the expense of what it encases, and plays a certain part even in the expression of the emotions."

I must pause right here, much as I admire his work, and much as I owe him, to quarrel with Mr. Lowell, who says that the people of the East, of the Far East at least, have never been led to regard the body as beautiful.

Is it possible that Mr. Lowell is unfamiliar with, or unappreciative of, the literature of Hindostan, the dramas of China, and the poems of Japan?

CHAPTER VI.

SLIGHT as is the visible part played by woman in Korea, yet there are an almost endless number of facts concerning her which are either significant or in themselves interesting. To me at least, woman, and the conditions of her life, together form the most interesting branch of the study of Korea. And even to those who take no deep interest in burning social questions, and whose interest in far-away lands scarcely exceeds an intelligent curiosity, any facts about Korean women must be especially interesting, I fancy, because those facts are less generally known, less easily known than almost any other facts connected with this wonderful peninsula, and its wonderful people. So I do not hesitate to devote another of my very limited number of chapters to the women of Korea.

Cosmetics are not, it is gratifying to say, a product of our Western civilization. They are greatly used all over the Orient. But in two particulars there is less to be said against the face-painting of Eastern women than there is to be said against the face-painting of the women of the West. In Asia, hair-oil, rouge, powder, khol for the eyes and eyebrows, and brilliant pigments for the lips, are put on frankly, and are as avowedly, and as sincerely, a seemly and decent adornment, and as much an item of being "dressed up," as is a silken petticoat or a jewelled necklet. Ladies of Asia "make up" more brazenly than the ladies of Europe, and their ugly, painted imitation is still less like the loveliness of nature than is the painted ugliness of ourselves when we do not feel that we have sufficient beauty of face to leave it unadorned. But the Eastern woman who "makes up" her face has no thought of deceiving anyone, or of obtaining masculine admiration or feminine envy under false pretences. Her painting is as much a matter of convention as is the Chinaman's wearing of his queue; and she lays on the thick layers of brilliant red and ghastly white as devoutly and as dutifully as she says her prayers. The other good word I have to say for the cosmetics of the Orient is this—they are infinitely less harmful than the cosmetics we are wont to

use in Europe. I know that. For, on the stage
I have tried both very thoroughly.

A well-to-do Korean woman usually has a
very interesting collection of hair-pins. They are
long, heavily ornamented, made of silver, of gold,
or of copper; more usually of silver. Some of
them are very beautiful, and some that I have
seen reminded me very much of the long silver
pins that are thrust through the braids of Italian
peasant women.

The well-to-do women, especially in the capital,
now very generally wear European under-cloth-
ing. They invariably wear a pouch which is
fastened by cords to their girdle. This is their
pocket, the only pocket they have, except their
sleeves, and in it they carry a tiger's claw for
luck, a small cushion of sachet, or a bottle of
thick, rich perfume, some of their favourite pieces
of jewellery, scissors usually, or a knife, two or
three of their most frequently used toilet implements, and almost invariably a small Korean
chess-board and chess-men. The board and the
pieces are often made of silver or even of gold.
Chess is, perhaps, the most popular of all Korea's
many games, and the Korean women of the
leisure class play it incessantly. The pocket also
contains, more likely than not, the official book
of female politeness; a book which every Korean

lady studies assiduously. But whatever this pocket contains or does not contain, it must by no means be without several charms, charms for good luck, charms for health, charms for wealth, and for any or every other good desirable under the Korean sun. Of its charms the most valuable is the tiger's claw. Mr. Griffis says, "Nor can the hardy mountaineer put into the hand of his bride a more eloquent proof of his valour than one of those weapons of a man-eater. It means even more than the edelweiss of other mountain lands." The tiger is probably the most dreaded foe of the Koreans. They fear it more than they fear China; hate it more than they hate Japan. The Chinese have a saying which so vividly pictures the tiger-Korean situation that I must quote it, though it has, I believe, already been quoted by every other European and the majority of Orientals who have ever written on Korea. It is this: "The Korean spends one half of the year hunting the tiger, and the other half in being hunted by him."

The hands of a Korean lady are always exquisitely kept, and usually loaded with rings, often with rings of very great value.

Among some classes of Korean women the dressing of their hair is the most important item of their toilet, and one skilled in ways Korean, and in signs of Korean rank, can very readily determine, from a glance at her coiffure, who and what a Korean woman is. The ladies of the court wear their hair in different prescribed ways. The geisha girls have an artistic fashion of their own, and a Korean woman servant, one part of whose duty is to fetch and to carry, makes out of the braids of her own hair an enormous cushion upon which she can carry with the greatest security a huge bundle, or a vast dish of food.

The men of no other race are so amply dowered with hats as are the men of Korea. Probably the women of no other civilized country are so badly off for head-gear as are the women of Chosön, and this is not, though we might easily fancy it to be, because those women are not supposed to walk or ride abroad. For innumerable years Korea has taken her fashions from China, changing them with the change of dynasty at Pekin. But for five hundred years the Koreans have failed to change the fashion of their hats, and they remain true to the style of head-gear which was in vogue when the present Korean dynasty came into power. When the present fashion in hats was imported from Pekin, just about five hundred years ago, the Koreans neglected to learn, or were unable to learn, what the women of China were wearing on their heads, or else the women of China were going bareheaded. The result was that Korean women, having discarded their previous head coverings, and receiving no authority from Pekin for the fashion of new ones, became hatless, and have been hatless ever since. The only hat the Korean women wear now is the folded dress which I have described before. There is indeed a jaunty, little embroidered cap not unlike a modified Turkish fez, or the glorious *capote* of a French *vivandière*, which is supposed to be at the disposal of any Korean woman who cares to assume it, but it has been adopted by the geisha girls, and so, of course, discarded by Korean ladies. Korean women used to wear a huge hat not unlike a small, flat, Chinese parasol. It was perched well up on and well to the back of their heads, and was surrounded by a rather fascinating silk fringe, through which they could see and be seen—a fringe that was, perhaps, as becoming to them as our white spotted veils are to us.

A few words here about divorce in Korea, for divorce is always a matter of more importance to a woman than to her husband. This is so in every country, because as yet in every country woman is more confined to her home, more dependent upon her home, and less free to go abroad at all seasons and under all circumstances than man is, and therefore less able to escape the daily torment of married unhappiness. In the United States, and in most European countries whose laws I have at all studied, the divorce laws are very much more in favour of woman than of man. In Korea the direct opposite is true. There is little or nothing for which a Korean woman can obtain a divorce, and there is little or nothing for which a Korean man cannot. Whether it is more to the credit of Korean woman or to the credit of Korean man far be it for me to say; but it is a very rare occurrence for a Korean husband to put aside his wife. The sanctity of the home circle, the inviolate maintenance of that home circle is more than a religion, more than an instinct with nine-tenths of the people of Asia. Their idea of a home circle may be more elastic than ours, but, as a rule, they abide by it almost with the courage of martyrs. The women must, and the men do. In one respect the divorce laws of Korea are more radical than the divorce laws of the West. Incompatibility of temper justifies divorce in Korea, and is the cause · of most Korean divorces. Truly nothing could be more sensible, more humane—provided one has no religious scruples—for even children lose more than they gain by living in an unhappy home. Incompatibility of temper may not be a sin, but it is the one difficulty in the path of married happiness, in Asia or in Europe, which can never be smoothed away. It is insurmountable, nor can you go around it. It seems to me that the only decent thing to do when you come upon it, again provided your conscience will let you, is to turn round and go back. A harsh word, a quick gesture, and many things that are many times worse can be forgiven readily enough, and almost forgotten, by people who have the common justice to judge not lest they be judged. But incompatibility of temper, that strange something which makes it impossible for me to teach my pet cat to eat or drink with my pet dog, ah! that is the marital thorn, the marriage plague, "past cure, past help, past hope." And I congratulate the law makers of Korea for recognizing it for what it is, and dealing with it as it should be dealt with. To be sure, if a Korean man and wife fail to get along, perpetually fail, the woman has no direct voice in the matter ; but if she and her husband agree together to untie the mistakenly-tied knot, he can very easily do so. And even in Korea a woman of average wit does not probably find it too difficult a task to make herself so very disagreeable that the husband may be brought to propose the separation which she secretly desires.

K

But where the Korean law seems to me very inconsistent is in not punishing, when the marriage is a failure, the geomancer who selected the wedding day. The method of this sage is so simple that it ought to be infallible. He adds the age of the bride to the age of the groom, and after determining which star rules the destiny of their united ages, he decrees that the wedding shall take place upon the day sacred to that star. How a day so chosen can ever fail to be auspicious, and to be the beginning of many days of uninterrupted happiness it is hard for a simple Western mind to understand. To do the geomancer justice, it is perhaps because of his occult wisdom that divorce plays so minor a part in Korean life.

One Korean law concerning women seems to me uniquely cruel. A woman may not die in the arms of a man, nor may a woman hold in her arms a man who is dying. Husbands and wives love each other sometimes—even in Korea. Mothers love their sons, the wide world over, and sons their mothers. Korean fathers yearn over their daughters, and are loved tenderly by those daughters in return. What a barbarous law! how infamous; how unworthy of the East or of the West! what a reflection upon humanity; what a stain upon Korea! That inferiority of sex (sex—

that unexplained accident of our physical existence), inferiority, real or imagined, should separate
man from wife, father from daughter, son from
mother, even by a hair's breadth, at the moment
when Death, the merciless, the relentless, pro-
nounces the great, and perhaps eternal separation!

Though a Korean woman nominally counts for
nothing in the ruling of her own household, and,
as far as the workings of the State go, does not
exist, she is invariably treated with the manner of respect; she is always addressed in what
is called "honorific language;" to her the
phraseology is used which is used to superiors,
people of age, or of literary eminence. A Korean
nobleman will step aside to let a Korean peasant
woman pass him on the street. The rooms of a
Korean woman are as sacred to her as a shrine
is to its image. Indeed, the rooms of his wife or of
his mother are the sanctuary of any Korean man
who breaks the law. Unless for treason or for
one other crime, he cannot be forced to leave those
rooms, and so long as he remains under the protection of his wife, and his wife's apartments, he
is secure from the officers of the law, and from the
penalties of his own misdemeanours.

It is often said that the men of the East regard
women not only as their inferiors, but as burdens,

as superfluous, useless, and despicable. This is a mistake, as large a mistake in speaking of Koreans as of any other Oriental race. The potence of sex, the impotence of either sex alone, is the great underlying thought of all Eastern philosophy, I had almost said, of all Oriental ethics. Which of the great Eastern religions ignores it, or passes it by lightly? Study the symbols in the old caves of India: read Confucius. Every educated Oriental believes that without women life would not only be impossible but worthless. They regard her sphere of usefulness as important as their own. An Oriental mother is almost an Oriental deity. This is as true in Korea as in China, in Japan, in Persia, in Hindostan, and in Burmah. The thinkers of Asia differ from us in what they regard as the most appropriate and the most essential spheres of women's usefulness, but they never ignore, nor do I think they underrate, the importance of woman's work. Mr. Griffis, who is not over partial to the Koreans (perhaps if he had ever lived among them he might have liked them better), himself says :—

" With the ethics of the Chinese came their philosophy, which is based on the dual system of the universe, and of which in Korean, *yum-yang* (positive and negative, active and passive, or male and female) is the expression. All things in heaven, earth, and man are the result of the inter-action of the *yum* (male or active principle), and the *yang* (female or passive principle). Even the metals and minerals in the earth are believed to be produced through the *yum-yang*, and to grow like plants or animals."

Even so clear, so cool, so sympathetic, so cultured, and best of all, so unbigoted an observer, a thinker, and a writer as Percival Lowell, seems to me to have blundered a little in his summing up of the position of woman in the East. He says :—

" The lower man's place in the scale of nations, the lower, relatively to his own, has always been that of woman. Woman, being physically less strong, naturally suffers where physical strength is made the basis of esteem. But as men have advanced in civilization, gradually a chivalrous regard has been paid the weaker, but fairer sex. Now, though the countries of the Far East have had their age of feudalism, in a general parallelism to those of the West, loyalty took the place of chivalry as one of its attendant feelings. At the point where woman elsewhere made her *début* upon the social stage, here she failed to appear ; and she has not done so since. The history of these races has been a history of man apart from any help from woman. To all social intents and purposes, woman has remained as she was when she followed as a slave in her Lord's wanderings. She is better fed now, better clothed, cleaner and more comfortable than she was ; but, relatively to the position of the people, no higher. She counts for nothing in the life of the race at the present time, as she has counted for nothing in it from the beginning."

That the history of the races of the Far East has been a history of man apart from any help of woman, I cannot understand Mr. Lowell's saying. He is evidently a man of very wide education, and he has lived in the Far East. Undoubtedly he has read the history of the Far East, and I cannot imagine the author of "Chosön, the Land of the Morning Calm," reading anything unintelligently. " That woman counts for nothing in the life of the race at the present time, as she has counted as nothing in it from the beginning!" Ah! yes, Mr. Lowell. She counts for a great deal. The tally of her influence may not be kept in the market-place, nor her power blazoned on the house-tops, but influence and power are there. She counts for a hundred things, and will count in every part of the globe, civilized or uncivilized, until Nature adopts a very different *modus operandi* from her present one. And in Korea, in China and Japan, woman counts above all for motherhood, and for the perpetuation of the race. And that she so counts must give her really great power among any race of men whose one eradicable religion is the worship of their ancestors, whose universal and insatiable ambition is to beget sons who may in turn worship them, and secure them a prosperous and a happy eternity.

There is much, very much that I deplore in the condition of woman in Korea. But once in a while woman gets the whip hand, and once in a very great while she has the wit to use it—and the nerve—even in Korea.

If it must be a canon of European literary good form to say very little, and to say it gingerly about Oriental polygamy, it has been a more than general custom among European writers to say nothing, nothing at least of any significance about the large class of Oriental women who stand outside the pale even of polygamy. There are some things that I think ought to be said about them; said now, when we are so very earnestly trying to understand the East, and, I hope, honestly striving to help the East. These things would come with more convention I know from the pen of a man, but I think they would come more appropriately from the pen of a woman, and I take upon myself the saying of them, in so far as I am able. I feel impelled to explain, as well as I can, the

exact social position, and the exact personally
mental attitude of the yoshiwara women of Japan,
the flower girls of China, and the geisha girls of
Korea. These three are sisters. They are
cousins, more or less close of kin, to the nautch
girls of India, and the posture girls of Burmah
and of Siam. But these three were born of one
father, and of one mother, and are the result of
one bringing up. What shall I call them? I
have no wish to use a harsh word that would offend
select European ears, nor will I use a harsh word
that would wrong and mis-describe them. I might
almost call them the understudies of the happier
women of the East; for in Asia's social life they
take the parts which ought, perhaps, to be played
by the harem-hidden wives and mothers of the
Orient. Those women, whose profession is publicity, are an important part of the social structure
of every Asiatic race I have known, except only
the Parsi race. To ignore their existence, when
travelling through Asia in person, or with pen, is
stupid. To slink by the strong position that they
hold in the East, the big significance of their firm
placement in the East, and the several lessons
they will not fail to teach us, if we do not fear to
learn, is prudish. To pass them by with a cry of
horror, and to condemn them as being what they
are not, is un-Christian and unjust.

For the men that mocked His agony and spat upon Him, Jesus claimed forgiveness, because " they knew not what they did." And certainly the professionally unfortunate women of the East have as little consciousness of degradation and of sin as they have of shame. There are many reasons why this is so, and I will try to state them. I am only less sorry for the homeless, nameless women of Asia, than I am for the homeless, nameless women of Europe. Perhaps this is the best place for me to say that I am making no plea for the profession of which I am writing. For the women who through folly, through ignorance, or who beneath the lash of that hardest of all taskmasters, circumstance, follow this nameless profession, I could easily find it in my heart to plead, and to plead, and to plead ; but not now nor here. What I wish to do now is to write frankly, freely, and truthfully of the women who make the seclusion and the sanctity of gentlewomen possible in the Far East.

After all's said and done, the social scales must balance or break, weight them as you will. And as the women of the Korean gentry are more secluded than those of any other Oriental gentry, so are the geisha girls of Chosön more interesting, more fascinating even than the yoshiwara women of Japan, and infinitely more so than the flower girls of China. Men living in the Far East, superior as they find the society of men to the society of men and women, tire of the perpetual society of men, and long to let down its intellectual average a bit by the introduction into it of women. Now the men of the East cannot possibly, from their point of view, bring their wives and daughters out from the safe shelter of home seclusion. But still they long for the mental, not to speak of the moral relaxation of woman's companionship, and so in the East a class of women has sprung up which is only very slightly analogous to the class of Western women from whom respectable Western women draw their skirts aside as they pass them in the Western streets.

Women seem to be an indispensable element of society after all. Social enjoyment without them is more or less a failure, at least in any very prolonged form. And in those countries where wives and mothers must veil their faces, a class has sprung into existence—a class whose exact social position is almost, if not quite, outside the pale of modern European comprehension.

The geisha of Korea, like the yoshiwara women of Japan, are sweetly pretty, soft-voiced, and charmingly mannered. And, like their sisters of Japan, they seem almost happy and quite dignified.

Perhaps indeed, they feel that they fulfil a national want—perform a national duty.

Companionship is the first and the chief thing required by an Oriental man from the women he pays to share some of the hours that he spends away from home. If the Hindoo, or Chinaman, or the Japanese, or the Korean man be poor, he has no leisure hours, and certainly cannot afford the illicit companionship which comes dear, and becomes dearer in the long run, all the world over. If he be well-to-do, the chances are that he has a bungalow or yamun running over with wives. Therefore, it is not for a common bestial satisfaction, but altogether for natural human companionship, that the men of the Far East so largely employ and so generously pay those Eastern women who have broken through the closed curtains and out of the sure safety of Oriental home-life, into the turmoil and the promiscuousness of society. Here, I must emphatically say, and it should be most emphatically remembered by anyone who is trying to understand the East: the nameless women of the East sin, but sin is neither their sole nor their chief occupation. To please, to amuse, to understand, and to companion men, mentally and socially, is their chief duty, their chief occupation, and their most earnest study. Sin follows, as sin has the grievous habit of following wherever people are human. But sin is neither the beginning nor the end, and I who can see no difference between a Korean wife and a Korean concubine, can see little or none between a Korean concubine and a Korean geisha. I am speaking of their morals, of course. The geisha girl is, as a rule, rather better educated than the concubine, better educated, quite possibly, than the wife ; for the geisha must make her way, and hold any position she gains, solely by personal talent, personal attractiveness, and personal attainments. Not for her to lay at the man's feet a son who may worship him into the most desirable corner of the Korean heaven ; only for her to please him while she is with him, to touch for him odd instruments and sing to them soft, weird songs, to shake the soft perfume of her hair across his cheek and the perfume of the flowers she wears upon the bowl of food, or of fish, or fruit she humbly places before him ; only for her to laugh at his humour, flat howsoever it may be ; only for her to applaud his ambitions, urge on his hopes, charm away his fears ; only for her to please ; never for her, save by accident, to be pleased. And that is the state of their sad fate in Europe, in Asia, in America, or in Africa : the women who give an everlasting all for a momentary nothing. Feminine unchastity is less degrading in the East

than in the West, and the unfortunate women of
the East are far less degraded than the unfortunate women of the West. There are three reasons
why this is so. In the Orient no woman is born
to immorality. In the Orient professional unchastity is not considered altogether immoral.
And immorality is not the only accomplishment
necessary for the professional success of an Asiatic
unfortunate.

In the Orient no woman is born to immorality.
The ranks of the immoral profession are recruited
from homes and from family circles that are
quite up to the Asiatic average, and an immoral
method of life is usually adopted by an Eastern
girl not from impulse, not from caprice, but from
a conviction that it is the surest and the most
sensible way for her to earn her living, and assist
in earning the living of her family. Her parents,
in all probability, share this conviction with her,
and nine times out of ten she makes her *début* in
the profession of sin after the elders of her family
have consulted earnestly together, and sifted, as
best they can, the probabilities and the possibilities of her future. So she starts into her
sad pilgrimage from a clean home, from clean
associations, and her instincts and herself are
clean and normal. She adopts sin gravely and
as a business; nor does it ever occur to her to

regard it as a self-indulgence; rather is it a penance, or an act of filial self-sacrifice.

In the East the life of a young girl is seldom wrecked by the misfortune which overtakes so many of our own girls. The social arrangements in the East prevent that, prevent it very effectually. When an Eastern girl takes upon herself a long martyrdom of public service she is at least of normal mind and whole of heart. Her nature, mental and moral, however it may be debased by her future life, is as yet unvitiated by any accumulation of ancestral wrong-doing. She may adopt sin for reasons that seem good and sufficient to herself and her parents, but she has no appetite for sin, no appetite inherited from her mother at least, so she has a fairer start than have the majority of unfortunate women in the Occident.

In the Orient professional unchastity is not considered altogether immoral. "There is nothing good or bad, but thinking makes it so." This may not be altogether true, but certainly there is a good deal of truth in it. The unfortunate women of the East have vastly more self-respect than have the unfortunate women of the West. They are not despised, and therefore they do not despise themselves; nor are they driven by the merciless scourges of public opinion to lower and coarser methods of life than those unavoidably

entailed by the profession they follow. Their
profession is not considered an honourable, an
elevating, nor an enviable one; but it is considered, by the people among whom they live,
as a useful and necessary and, within certain loose
limits, an honest one. This makes it possible
for them to lead lives of comparative respectability, and to enjoy frankly, fearlessly, and purely
some of the best things of life. The flowers that
grow about their houses, and the wonderful skies
that canopy their countries, convey to them no word
of reproach. They gather the blossoms as inno-
cently, and they smile back at the smiling heavens
as unshamedly as does any maiden in the East.

If one gives a dog a sufficiently bad name it
becomes almost righteous to hang him. The
peoples of the Orient spare their unfortunate
women unnecessary contumely. And this is the
second reason why those women are better, less
deplorable, individually and collectively, than are
such women in Europe or America. This seems
to me another instance of Asiatic justice and
good sense. Why such women, and such women
alone, should be blamed for an existing state of
general immorality I cannot imagine. They are
not responsible for it, though, of course, they
help to perpetuate it. They take to life's sad
market-place wares for which they know there

is a demand. They supply the demand ; but they do not create it.

Immorality is not the only accomplishment necessary for the professional success of an Asiatic unfortunate. As I have said, companionship is the chief return an Eastern man expects and exacts for the coin that he throws into the lap of a light woman. The loose women of the East must be educated, and that they are educated makes it possible for them to spend many hours of each day in wholesome, refining occupations—occupations which are closed to the great mass of European unfortunates.

To recapitulate, the women of whom I am writing are of a better grade than are such women in the West, because in the East those women come from respectable homes and have memories of innocent and happy childhoods. Secondly, because they are so regarded in the East that they need not altogether part with self-respect ; and lastly, because education and refinement are not only possible to them, but necessary to them, and because the majority of their professional hours are passed in conversation or with music, and are altogether free from coarseness.

I have spoken of these women as being out of the pale of matrimony. This is true, I believe, in China and in Korea, and in most other Oriental countries; but it is not at all true in Japan. It used to be in Japan an ordinary occurrence, and even now it is not, I think, unusual for a girl to sell herself for a stated period of time into the horrible slavery of a tea-house, or become for some definite number of years the mistress of a well-to-do man. This is often done to earn enough money to pay some debt of family honour, to redeem the pledged word of a father or of a brother. The girl who does it is considered anything and everything rather than a bad woman. She returns to her native village, or to her father's house, when the time of her servitude has expired, and she is received with every possible sign of honourable welcome, and is pointed out then and thereafter as an example of daughterly perfection, and of virtuous womanhood. She marries as readily and as well as any of her girl friends, and her past is not regarded as to her detriment either by her husband or his family. This practice is more common among the poor than among the rich. But there are women of very high position in Japan who have had this terrible experience, and who have survived it, mentally and morally.

There is, of course, in Japan a large number of women who adopt immorality when they are very young, and who never put it aside. They are called yoshiwara women. In the old times they lived apart, not only in quarters of the town set aside for them, but in quarters that were enwalled, and through the gateways of which they could not pass without permission—permission that was not too readily granted. Even now there are streets set apart in almost every Oriental city— set apart for the occupancy of unfortunate women. The roads and the byways of Japan are sprinkled with tea-houses, and in almost every tea-house there are two or more yoshiwara women. These tea-houses are models of cleanliness, are usually pretty in situation, and always artistically furnished. The tea, cakes, and sweets sold in them are almost invariably delicious. The girls who are supposed to be the chief attraction of the tea-houses are rather brazen as a rule, far more so than the flower-girls of China, or the geisha girls of Korea, but it is a very butterfly sort of brazenness. Their manners are so pretty, their movements so bird-like, and their voices so tinkling and silvery, that it seems rather unfair to criticize them for being somewhat over-emphatic in what they say and do, and in how they say and do it.

I remember one warm afternoon in Kobe, I was in my jinrickshaw and several miles from home. I was tired, very thirsty, and my four-year-old boy, who was with me, assured me that he could not

live much longer unless he had something to eat.
I stopped at a tea-house—a pretty, carved,
lantern-hung place that was perched on the hill-
side, not very far from the marvellous waterfall.
I had not been very long in Japan, and had no
idea that I was making a social blunder, but I
noticed that my jinrickskaw coolie looked dis-
turbed and dubious. Two Japanese girls sat on
the verandah; one was smoking a long silver pipe,
and the other was picking whispered music from
a diminutive white guitar. One girl wore a
kimono of pale green crêpe, brocaded with pink
apple-blossoms; the other girl's kimono was of
dark, bright blue, but it was almost covered with
huge yellow roses. Both girls wore the ordinary
Japanese sash, had their hair elaborately dressed,
and were rather loaded with jewellery. Through
the openings of their kimonos peeped the edges of
sundry other garments, all of crêpe or of silk, and
all brilliantly coloured. They laughed and nodded
as I came up the steps, and when I said that my
boy and I were hungry and thirsty, one of them
rose and led me into the house. We passed
through a fair-sized room in which half a dozen
European men, one of whom I happened to know,
and as many Japanese girls were feasting rather
merrily. The girls looked at me with considerable good-natured amusement; the European

men looked at me in most considerable surprise. Baby and I were taken into a dainty little room which really was not big enough for more than two, and there were given quite a delightful luncheon. The girl who had showed us in waited upon us gravely and most attentively, and with admirable patience, for we were both hungry, very hungry, and thirsty, very thirsty. I found out afterwards that it was the first time she had poured afternoon tea for one of her own sex, and that I had made a most unfortunate mistake in going into the tea-house at all. But the girl who served us treated me and herself with perfect respect.

Respectable Japanese women wear the quietest of colours, in public at least. Bright flowers, glittering jewellery, and gaudy garments are the avowed livery of the yoshiwara women. They are pretty as a rule—these women—prettier even than the run of Japanese women ; for in Japan personal beauty is considered one of the indispensable attributes of women who would lead a life of remunerative idleness.

The flower-girls of China are in most ways more to be pitied than the yoshiwara women of Japan. They are not as a rule so well educated, nor so comfortably housed, and though treated with a good deal of allowance, and collectively taken, as a matter of course, their position is neither so assured, nor the circumstances of their lives so endurable as are those of the Japanese girls. The breaking of the seventh commandment may be as common in China as it is in Korea or Japan, but it is not so lightly regarded, and the flower-girls are almost without exception the children of extreme poverty. And a Chinese woman who has once lived in a house of ill-fame can never go back to even apparent respectability. This is not so in the Straits Settlements, where there are very many Chinamen and very few Chinese women. In Singapore and in Penang Chinese girls who have been sent from China for immoral purposes very frequently marry well, and pass the rest of their lives in security and comfort. But in China I fancy that this never happens.

The Chinaman is the most domesticated of the men of the East, and the least fond of general society. He does not go to the houses of the flower-girls for society, for companionship, not at least in any quiet and unobjectionable sense, nor so commonly as do Korean and Japanese men. The Chinese flower-girl, except the very lowest type, is taught to sing, to play on several instruments, to heat wine and to spice it, to prepare delicacies and table dainties, and to serve a feast.

She is taught to keep herself as good-looking from a Chinese standpoint as possible. But this is usually the list of her accomplishments, the limit of her education, and she is vastly ignorant compared to the women who dwell in the house of the man who patronizes her. Many of these Chinese women live outside the gates of Chinese cities. Thousands of them live in little boats that are called "flower-boats" and off of which they seldom go. The "flower-boats" of Canton are a most distinctive feature of that most distinctly quaint place. Shortly before the declaration of war between China and Japan, the following telegram was sent from Hong Kong :—

"A terrible fire has occurred on the Canton river among the flower-boats which crowd the surface and form the permanent dwelling of a large number of the population. Hundreds of the flower-boats were destroyed, and fully one thousand natives must have perished.

"The boats were moored stem and stern in rows, and the flames spread with such rapidity that many of the craft were fully alight and their occupants overcome before they could cut the boats from their moorings and push them out into the open water."

As if poor China were not in trouble enough just then, with a terrible plague still in rather full swing, and with war and with rumours of war, but must needs go and set herself on fire!

I don't in the least doubt that there was a terrible fire on the Canton river, and that over a thousand human creatures perished in the flames. Such a catastrophe is by no means unprecedented in China, and most especially in Canton. But I do doubt that the fire broke out among the flower-boats. In the first place the flower-boats do not crowd the surface of the Canton river. In the second place they do not form the permanent dwelling of a large number of the population. I think that the sender of the dispatch, or one of the operators through whose hands it passed, must have confused flower-boats, sampans and Chinese cargo-boats.

The flower-boats are not in a crowded part of the river. They are moored quite by themselves at the wide mouth of the river and some little distance from the city. They are together, but not painfully near. No families dwell upon them. They are occupied solely by the flower-girls and their servants, and at night their decks and cabins swarm with rich and dissipated Chinamen. Then their windows are brilliant with light, their decks are bright with fanciful lanterns, and they are noisy with laughter and the tinkling of strange stringed instruments, and they smell of hot

samshu. Not the sort of place in which one would expect flowers to thrive! Alas! the flowers on those boats are human flowers. They are painted with brilliant colours, but not by the hand of nature.

The girls who live there are not vendors of buds and blossoms. "Flower-girl" is the name by which the over chivalrous Chinamen designate a woman who is professionally unchaste.

On the opposite side of the river's mouth, but still farther from the city, are moored the miserable boats of the lepers. The saddest of sins and the saddest of diseases are within sight of each other. Both are outside the pale of Chinese society. Both are excluded from Cantonese citizenship.

Because of their isolation, I doubt that the recent fire occurred among the flower-boats. But among the small cargo-boats, among the thickly huddled sampans! Yes; likely enough there.

Surely it is horrible enough to live all one's life in a Chinese sampan or in a small junk, without being burnt to death into the bargain. Drowning, now, is a very common occurrence on a Chinese river. No one takes much notice of that in Canton. To be sure the mothers put crude, home-made life preservers on their babies, or tie a long rope about their little yellow waists, fastening the other end firmly to the boat. So if a Chinese baby falls overboard (as it usually does two or three times a day), it has a very fair chance of floating or being hauled back. But the adults must take their chances, and extraordinary numbers of them manage to tumble into a watery grave. Hundreds of Chinese are born in sampans, live in sampans, die in sampans. Yet almost none of them can swim.

For one thing the canals and rivers are too crowded. There is no room for them to swim in. For another thing they have no time to learn how to swim. It's all work and no play to most of the sampan dwellers.

Think of a family of ten or twelve, or even more, who live in a one-roomed boat, a boat not many times the size of a big row-boat. Think what their family life must be. And they are only one of myriad families. They live in a quarter denser than the densest of the crowded city streets. Think of the stench! Think of the din! Small wonder that they take drowning almost tranquilly. But to be burnt to death! That's another matter. Even stolid Chinese philosophy may be expected to shrink from that. Think of being burned to death in a boat, on a river, and yet not being able to drown one's death agony in the cooling water, because every inch of the water's surface was covered with hundreds of other burning humans!

Such things happen not infrequently in China, and yet hundreds and hundreds of thousands of Chinese continue to live in the sampans and in the cargo-boats. They must live there. There is no place else for them to live; unless they leave China, and few of them have the wish to do that: none of them have the means. Their dire poverty drives them into the wretched boats and imprisons them there, and there they must remain until they die of old age, of overwork, of starvation, or die by drowning or fire, as the case may be. And the children born and bred on those boats! No wonder that when the boys are grown to manhood many of them are only fit to hide themselves within the leper-boats; that when the girls are grown to womanhood very many elect to have the comparative luxury of the flower-boats!

The Korean geisha probably gets more enjoyment out of life and is less conscious of wrongdoing than is the woman of any other race who follows the same profession. It follows naturally enough that the race whose standard of sexual morality is lowest, regards women of unchaste lives more leniently than does any other race. Then, too, the seclusion of Korean ladies is more rigid than the seclusion of the gentlewomen of any other Asiatic country. This makes the men of Korea entirely dependent upon the geisha girls for any outside female companionship, and the Korean man is very sociable, very fond of good times, and if he can afford it, apt to make not only a plaything, but rather a friend out of the girl whose profession it is to be amusing, entertaining and cheerful, at so much an hour.

The word geisha is a Japanese word, and it signifies " accomplished person." The Korean word for the class of women of whom I am writing is ki-saing; but they are generally called geisha. The Japanese yoshiwara women are called geisha, as often as anything else.

In proportion to the populations of the two countries there are far fewer geisha in Korea than in Japan, but this is solely, I think, because Korea is so much poorer than Japan ; for nowhere are women of their profession more appreciated, more esteemed, and treated by men more on an equality than they are in Chosön. The Korean geisha is systematically and carefully trained for her intended profession. Several years are occupied by her education, and not until she is proficient in singing, in dancing, in reciting, in the playing of many instruments, in repartee, in the pouring of wine, in the filling and lighting of pipes, in making herself generally useful at feasts and festivals, and above all, in being good-natured, is she allowed to ply her trade. In or near every large Korean city are picturesque little buildings called " pleasure-houses." They are very like the tea-houses of Japan. They are usually built in some secluded spot, and are surrounded by the brilliance of flowers, and half hidden beneath the shadow of trees. They are scantily but artistically furnished, and are running over with tea and sweetmeats and girls.

The geisha of the King are, of course, the flower of the profession, and are dressed even more elaborately than the ordinary geisha, which is quite superfluous. They remind one very much, both in manner and in habit, of the posture girls of Burmah, and the European who was a looker-on at a festival in Li Hsi's palace might easily fancy that when Thebaw was dethroned, his posture girls, whose occupation was of course then gone, had fled *en masse* to the court at Söul. Most Asiatic dances are slow. Probably the slowest of them all is the dance of the Korean geisha. Like all the dances of the Far East, with which I am at all familiar, it is absolutely free from vulgarity, or from suggested coarseness. The geisha herself is covered and covered from throat to ankle. It would be imprudent to say how many dresses she usually wears at once. She dresses in silk and in glimmering tissues. Before dancing she usually takes off two or three of her gowns, and tucks up the trains of the robes she still wears, but even so she is very much dressed, and a thoroughly well-clad person. In winter she wears bands of costly fur on her jaunty little cap, and an edge of the same fur about her delightful little jacket of fine cashmere, or of silk. She wears most brilliant colours, and all her garments are perfumed and exquisitely clean. Indeed, cleanliness must be her ideal of godliness. At least, it is the only godliness she knows, and, save the virtue of amiability, the only virtue she would be ashamed to lack. Her parents are poor, always very poor, and she is pretty, always very pretty. It is this prettiness which causes her almost from her baby-hood to be destined for the amusement profession. It makes her suitable for that profession, and ensures her probable success in it. Her parents gladly set her aside from the toilers of the family, and she is given every possible advantage of mind and person. So she is insured a life of ease, and even of comparative luxury. She is a blooming, gladsome thing, with gleaming eyes, and laughing lips, and happy dancing feet. She looks like some marvellous human flower when you meet her in the streets of Söul, and forms an indescribable contrast to the draggled crowds that draw apart to let her pass as she goes on her laughing way to her well-paid work.

The geisha girls are greatly in demand for picnics, and in the summer often spend days in the cool, fragrant woods, playing for, reciting to, and feasting with some merry party of pleasure-makers. If their services are required at a Korean feast they usually slip in one by one when the meal is more than half done. The host and his guests make room for them, and each girl seats herself near to a man whose attendant she thus becomes for the entire evening. They pour wine for the men, and see that all their wants and creature comforts are well looked after. They do not eat unless the men voluntarily feed them. To feed them is to give them a great mark of favour, and it would be the worst of bad form for them to refuse any morsel so offered. After the feast they sing and dance in turn and together. They recite love stories and ballads, and strum industriously away upon funny Korean instruments. Their singing is very plaintive: as sad as any earthly music, but it is not sweet nor pleasing to European ears. The geisha are often employed to perform before private families, and not unfrequently before the harems of rich men or mandarins. To introduce them for an evening into the most respectable family circle is regarded as the best of good taste.   Some of these girls live together, many of them live, nominally at least, in the homes of their own childhood.   They form strange contrasts to their sisters of approximately the same age, whose lives have been lives of virtue and incessant work.

The geisha never by any chance become familiar with, or are treated familiarly by the women of the harems into which they are occasionally introduced, and yet some of them are not unchaste in their personal lives.   This, however, is of course very exceptional.   Occasionally the geisha becomes the concubine of a man of position, or the personal attendant of a man of wealth.   When old age, that dread foe of woman the wide world over, creeps upon them, they become the teachers of the girls who are ambitious to become geisha.

No geisha girl expects to be entertained. It is her business to entertain.   The moment she enters the presence of her employer or employers, she takes unobtrusively the thorough charge of the social side of the function.   She makes herself useful and amusing, and agreeable in every possible way, and apparently has no thought of self.   Often a large party of Korean gentlemen will go for a stay of some days to one of the monasteries that still dot the Korean hillsides.   They usually take with them an incredible train of servants, and a number of geisha. Rare times they have on these excursions, and rare welcome do the monks give them. The monks and the servants and the geisha devote themselves to the lords of the situation. And the Korean man who goes picnicking to a Korean monastery probably has as good a time as any reveller in the East.

Such are the Magdalenes of the far Orient! To be pitied, to be deeply pitied, but to be less pitied than the Magdalenes of the West, for they are better housed, better treated, and less conscious of their misfortune. There is, I think, a good deal worth pondering over in the way the peoples of Asia deal with the great social sin—a sin from which our human race can scarcely hope for redemption, unless indeed,—

> " Heaven peep through the blanket of the dark,
> To cry, Hold, hold !"

CHAPTER VII.

KOREAN ARCHITECTURE.

WHAT her dress is to woman, his dwelling is to man. I am speaking, of course, of average man and of average woman. What she wears indicates what she is, and is the most natural, the most unconscious, and the most common expression of her individuality, and of her character. She, her very self, peeps from beneath the laces at her neck. The house in which he lives shelters his women and his young; the buildings which he erects, or helps to erect, indicate who and what he is, and are the most natural, the most unconscious, and the most common expression of his individuality, and of his character; and we may see him as he really is, in his roof, his door-step, and, in brief, in the exterior and the interior of his home.

It is this, its revelation of mankind, which makes architecture so intensely interesting a study, the most interesting, I often think, of all the studies of the inanimate. Not for their grace of outline, not for their beauty of colour, not for their artistic consistency, not for their happy placement, are the great buildings of this world supremely interesting to us; but for the glimpses they give us into the souls, the lives of the men who have reared them.

Of more recent years records have been made and preserved of the doings of most of the civilized peoples, but, beyond a doubt, many such records made in olden times have been irretrievably lost, and many a page of history—a page clear and convincing to us to-day—would have been lost to us for ever were it not for the silent but indisputable testimony of old buildings : ruined houses, scraps of temples, broken bridges, crumbling towers, and grotesque caves.

It is impossible to speak of Korean architecture without speaking of Chinese architecture, and of Japanese architecture. And it is so impossible to separate the architecture of Korea from either the architecture of China, or the architecture of Japan, that one has a very convenient excuse for writing of the architecture of Korea as it visibly is, and for writing little or nothing of what it means. Korean architecture, in all its best phases, is purely Tartar. Chinese architecture is largely Tartar. But China, in architecture, as in ethics, and as in sociology, is at heart more or less Mongolian. China has been ridden under, not exterminated, by Tartar supremacy. Japanese architecture is Tartar, but it is very many other things, and the charitable mantle of Japanese art is so all-covering, and her artists have graciously adopted the art-methods of so many different peoples, that it is quite impossible to say whether Tartar influence is the parent or the powerful adopted child of Japanese art.

For convenience, I will divide Korean architecture into the architecture of the poor and the architecture of the rich. Korean hovels are like most other hovels. Extreme poverty goes rather naked the wide world over, and the Korean poor live in houses of mud, roofed with leaves; and if the leaves and the mud give out they have holes in their roofs instead of chimneys.

Korean hovels, Korean houses, and Korean palaces have many characteristics in common, characteristics which are climatic and racial. Let us peep first at the homes of the Korean poor. The home of a poor Korean, dwell he in a Korean city, dwell he in a Korean village, or dwell he desperately perched upon the rocky side of a Korean mountain, is a house of one story—that is, of one story in which people live. Above is a thin sort of attic in which grains and other pro-

visions are stored, and beneath is a fairly thick
sort of basement in which heat is bred, from
which heat is generated. Like all other Korean
houses the interior of this house is lined with
paper. It has a paper roof, paper floor, or floor-
cloth, and paper walls. The walls slide back or
lift up, or are in one of several other ways got rid
of, in the summer ; but they are walls for all that,
no less walls because they are also windows and
doors. Paper is the chief feature of every ordinary
Korean house ; and to say that is to say a great
deal for paper: because the cold of a Korean
winter is excessive, is far beyond the cold of the
winter in which I write. In every Korean house,
be it the house of prince or of pauper, there is
what seems to be at first sight, to European eyes,
a paucity of furniture. There is nothing more
significant of the difference between the simple
artisticness of the East and the elaborate inart-
isticness of the West than the way in which
Western rooms are crowded with inanimate
unnecessaries, and the way in which Eastern
rooms are sparsely supplemented with inanimate
necessaries.

I had afternoon tea yesterday with a friend
who loves me so well, and whom I so well love,
that I am sure she will forgive me for drawing, to
her disadvantage, a comparison between her

drawing-room and the drawing-room of a Korean man, or the boudoir of a Korean woman. I never go into my friend's drawing-room without feeling a thrill of admiration for the nice way in which her butler avoids knocking over one of a pair of priceless vases, which were stolen from Pekin about the time that Sir Harry Parkes and Sir Henry Loch were rather inconveniently imprisoned there. I creep in, as gracefully as I can, between the butler and the two priceless blue things. I cross a bit to the left, to avoid a malachite table crowded with silver pigs (some of them so little that they would look lost on a threepenny-bit, some of them a foot or more long) ; then I cross to the right, to avoid a wonderful teak-wood cabinet of no particular style, that looks very staggery beneath a multitude of tea-pots—tea-pots most of which are not interesting in themselves, and none of which are interesting in their common conglomeration. Then I almost trip over the wool of a slaughtered Persian lamb, and I just save myself from tumbling into a Louis Quinze chair, and so I work my way through the ages—through the races, until I reach my hostess, who, like myself and everyone else there, is in nice, new, nineteenth-century, ugly raiment. There may be space in. this London drawing-room for her, for me, and for all the other ordinary folk which are gathered together, because we are very much alike, but there is not room for all the chairs, and the tables, and half the other pieces of furniture, because no two of them are alike. We humans are used to fashionable crushes, but I think it is a shame not to give the furniture room to breathe.

Let us peep into a Korean drawing-room. A long cool place. There is a padded quilt, probably covered with silk, in one corner. The host sits on that, and any guests that come to him. If the weather be cold, and the host be rich, a brazier of charcoal usually stands in another corner. There is a small table, or perhaps there are two, with writing and painting materials. Unless the house be one of dire poverty there is, at one end of the room, a chest of drawers or a buffet, or a sideboard, or something of that sort : a huge piece of furniture made out of more or less costly woods, fitted with drawers and doors, and embellished with metal handles. The handles, or the clasps, or the locks are made in the shape of butterflies, for the butterfly is a very favourite expression of Korean artistic outline. When it is time to eat, a table is brought in for the host and one for each of his guests—a table a foot or two high, and just about as square as high. Upon this, small dishes of food are placed, and small but often-filled cups of drink. When the meal is over, the tables and the dishes and the remnants of meat and of liquor (but there are not often many of either) are taken away.

In an ordinary Korean house there is little or no other furniture. A screen perhaps, precious for its decorations, and for the carvings of its frame, and three or four pictures—pictures distinctly Korean, but I assure you by no means inartistic. I can think of nothing else that ordinarily furnishes a Korean room, except the quaintly clad people, and the sunshine that comes in almost iridescently—it shines through windows of so many different colours : windows of paper. The colour of the light depends entirely upon the colour and the texture of the paper through which it comes. A Korean bed-room is very like a Korean sitting-room. The quilt upon which a Korean sits through the day is the same as, or very like, the quilt upon which he sleeps at night. Tiger skins are also greatly used for floor rugs and bed coverings.

To stray a moment from the exact subject of architecture. The Koreans wear, I believe, very much the same clothes in day as in night. Indeed, I believe that the Korean changes his or her garments for five reasons only : to eat, to put on new clothes when the old ones are worn out, to have the clothes she or he is wearing washed, to put on his or her best clothes in celebration of some festival or other ceremonial, and to go into mourning. Firstly and foremost, a Korean undresses to eat. They are not civilized enough, the people of Chosön, to array themselves for feeding time. They do not deny their relationship with other hungry mammals. When they are hungry they eat. When they are thirsty they drink, and to be truthful, their hunger and their thirst is usually enormous, and of long endurance. They are neither ashamed of their hunger nor of their thirst, for they appease neither before going to a feast. Indeed, to gorge oneself is considered the acme of Korean elegance, and it is the one elegance in which all Koreans, rich and poor, young and old, male and female, prince and peasant, indulge themselves on every possible or semi-possible occasion. And that they may eat the utmost possible morsel, they loosen their garments before they sit down to the feast.

But I was speaking of the houses of the Korean poor. Perhaps it is rather inappropriate to speak of banquets in connection with them ; yet, except among the most abjectly poverty-stricken, banquets are held sometimes (at marriages, on birthdays, on feast-days, and on lucky-days, if possible) in every Korean home.

Only Koreans of certain position are allowed to cover their roofs with tiles. A peasant's roof is almost invariably thatched with straw or grass. Every Korean house contains but one room, or, to state it differently, every Korean room, excepting for a door opening into another house or room, is in itself a complete house. It has a roof of its own, and four walls of its own, and is in every way independent of any other rooms or houses, which may form other parts of its owner's dwelling. When inside a Korean dwelling one may fancy oneself in a suite of apartments opening into each other, that is, of course, if a certain number of the paper walls are opened. From the outside of a Korean dwelling, one seems to be looking at a collection of more or less closely built, but entirely independent houses. The position of woman being what it is, even the poorest Korean house has, or ought to have, more than one room. This peculiarity; this similarity between exteriors and interiors, makes Korean architecture uniquely picturesque, and public buildings and the dwellings of the rich supremely so. Indeed, the better class of houses often have not only a roof to each room, but·two or three roofs to each room. Now a Korean roof, to my mind, is the most beautiful roof in the world. It is Chinese in general character, and slopes from the ridge pole in graceful concave curves. Except in the houses of the poor it is tiled. The tiles overlap each other, are unevenly curved, and rest upon a foundation of earth. In the course of a few seasons a Korean roof breaks into bud, and into blossom. Perhaps a great patch of odd blue flowers covers one-half of the roof, perfuming the air for many yards. Perhaps quaint crimson tulips lift their happy heads between every few tiles. Wild pinks, forget-me-nots, and orchids mingle on one roof, and another roof glitters in the sunshine like gold because it is the bed of a thousand yellow sun-lilies.

Imagine an old Korean monastery which is backgrounded by hills, some of them covered with verdure, and some of them naked rocks, rocks that are broken here and there by patches and cracks of hardy flowers. In the distance, we hear the melodious drip of some gentle waterfall. Nearer we hear the full-throated soprano of the larks. And a dozen other birds, green and blue, and purple, and grey with breasts of yellow, fly from their nests in the teak-wood trees, to drink the sweet blood of the blooming iris. The monastery has a score or more of houses, each rambling from some other. The monastery is low and porticoed, and the doors, which are also its windows and its walls, are slid back in the grooves, and our view of each of the many interiors is only obstructed by the eight square posts which are the only permanent walls of a Korean building. Inside we catch a glimmer of metallic Buddhas, and hear the careless Sanskrit sing-song of the monks. In the courtyard stands a great brass Korean bell or gong, and the stick with which it is struck lies beside it. A huge glimmering gong is this; to call the brethren to prayer and to rice. Around the edges of the monastery's roofs runs a peculiar shell-like beading, which is a distinction of a sacred or religious edifice. The roof was a dark brown once, but the tiles, those that have not been broken away, have grown purple and blue, softened by time and blighted by weather. Where the tiles have crumbled away, and over many tiles that have not yet succumbed to decay, honey-suckles, yellow and buff, and white and rose-coloured, are creeping and tangling themselves with great, green ropes that are heavy with gourds—gourds that are little and pale, and gourds that are big and golden and speckled.

Or let us look at some one of the king's many houses. Its round columns and its square rafters are lacquered and crimson. Its paper walls are as fine and as polished as silk. Innumerable steps lead up to it, and it is almost heavy with carvings. Three roofs shelter it, and look like a tent with an awning above an awning. Each roof is a bed of flowers that are brilliant and fragrant—flowers among which birds that are splendid of feather, and sweet of throat, make their nests. But the birds and the flowers are not the only denizens of the typical Korean roof. Effigies in mud, in bronze, or in wood squat on the ridges. They look a little like monkeys, very little like men, and some of them very much like pigs. They are absurd and impossible to a degree, and yet, for all that, they are rather life-like, and, on a weird moonlight night, decidedly startling. These are the protectors of the houses; and what the scarecrow which the European or American farmer manufactures out of his oldest trousers, his most ragged coat, and his most disreputable hat, is to the blackbirds and the crows of the Occident, these grotesque figures are to the evil spirits of Korea. They frighten away the devils, the gods of misfortune, and the demons of disease that would fain light upon the roofs, and curse the dwellers of the houses. Socially they belong with the demons and the imps and the witches, with the monks and the nuns, and the hundred other personages of Korea's queer religious or irreligious spiritualistic community. But physically they are a striking and a fascinating detail of Korea's remarkable architecture.

I have spoken of the khans, which are the furnaces of the Korean houses. They are not altogether underground, and so every Korean house rests, as it were, upon a pedestal—a pedestal of stone or of earth. But the house is almost never built of stone. Wood and paper are its only materials, and few of the countries in the world are richer in woods, and no country is so rich in paper as Korea.

The fame of Korea's paper is more world-wide than the fame of any other Korean product. But admirable as it is, superior for many purposes as it is to all other papers, it is really for her woods, and for their quality, that Korea should be noted more than for any other thing which she grows or manufactures. Bamboo is there, of course, in abundance, and abundantly used. Find me the country in Asia where bamboo does not grow, and I'll vow to you that that country has been an iceberg and in some strange way become detached from its anchorage at the North Pole, drifted down to the southern seas, and after centuries become overgrown with all sorts of green and gay things, and so come to think itself, and to be thought, a part of the Orient. When I say that bamboo grows in Korea I am saying that Korea is in Asia, and I am saying no more. The temples, the palaces, the shrines, and the lumber-yards of China and Japan were for many years, and now largely are, dependent for the most choice of their woods upon the forests of Korea. And many of the most valued of the tree species in Japan have sprung up from seeds that were gathered in Chosön. In the palaces, and in the joss-houses of Pekin, and in the famous temples of Tokio and Kioto, columns and ceilings of especial beauty and of great value, commercially and artistically, have been hewn from trees that grew in Korea. Korea is rich in willow, in fur, in persimmon, in chestnut, and in pine—pine which the Chinese prefer above all other woods for many of the parts of waggons, boats, and ships. Korea is rich in ash, in hornbeam, in elm, and in a dozen other hard, very hard, enduring timbers. The flag that flies above the yamun of a Chinese mandarin is in all probability attached to a pole of Korean wood, and, beyond doubt, the white flags that so recently fluttered upon the ill-fated ships outside the forts of Wei-Hai-Wei, had not those ships been built in Europe, would have made their signals of defeat from the top of what once had been trees in Chei-chel-sang or in Hoang-hai. Korea is splendid with oaks, and with maples, and is well supplied with larch and with holly. And at one season of the year many of her hill-slopes are purple with mulberries. The juniper-tree grows there in vast numbers ; the cork-tree and the Korean varnish-tree, from the sap of which comes the golden-hued lacquer, which is one of the important materials of Korean art. This sap is poisonous, so poisonous that the men who work with it are paid above the rates usually received by Korean art-artisans. There is another tree in Korea which has so disagreeable a name that I won't name it, but from it a very fine white wax is extracted. And there are trees that are pricked for the oil that gushes from them—oil from which one of the great national drinks—a hot, peppery drink—is made, and which is almost the only oil used in the toilet of a Korean woman.

So the Korean architect and the Korean builder have the choice of many woods in the erecting of Korean edifices. A marvellous species of oak grows plentifully in Korea—oak whose timbers have been known, and proved to have been, under water for a century at least, and without decaying. But perhaps the most famous of the woods of Korea are the wonderful red and black woods that grow on the island of Quelpaert.

Paper forms a larger part, and is almost as indestructible a part of the Korean house as is wood. This paper is made from cotton—cotton whose fibre is exceptionally long, soft, satiny, and fine. Most Korean papers are beautiful to look at, delightful to touch, and incredibly strong. It is almost impossible to tear them, especially when they are oiled as they are for all architectural purposes. The varieties of Korean papers are almost endless. One kind is an excellent substitute for cloth, and is used for the making of garments, and for linings, and in many ways it takes the place of leather, of woods, and of metals, and of all sorts of woollen things. There is a very thick paper which is made from the bark of the mulberry-tree. It is soft and pliable, and is as glazed as satin. It is almost, if not quite, the most easily washed substance I have ever seen, and is *par excellence* the Korean choice for table-cloths.

Glass is almost unknown in Korea, and until recent years was quite unknown there. And as we are all very apt to prize most that with which we are least familiar, and the use of which we least understand, so Koreans set great value upon glass. Old bottles, washed ashore from some European shipwreck, often form the most prized bric-a-brac in a mandarin's dwelling, and any Korean who can get a square foot or two of glass to insert in one of the paper windows of his house is a very proud householder indeed.

In the house of a noble the front or outer apartment is used as a reception-room. Here his friends and acquaintances (indeed, all whose rank entitle them to mingle with him) gather night after night for gossip, for tobacco, and for drink. These rooms take the place of clubs, of bar-rooms, and of the smoking-rooms of hotels, all of which are unknown in Korea.

Background and environments are so studied by every architect in the Far East that landscape-gardening may almost be said to be a part of Korean architecture. No Korean building of any importance lacks courtyards, lotus ponds, groves of trees, and tangles of flowers, through all of which are scattered elaborate little summer-houses. And what the rich Korean does for the surroundings of his house and his city, nature almost invariably does for the surroundings of the house of the poor Korean, who does not live in one of the crowded cities. The Korean hut is sometimes half covered with vines, and is altogether cool and delightful from the shade and the perfume of trees that are heavy with flowers, with fruits, and with nuts. No Korean need be roofless. If a house be burned down, or be blown down, the entire community are more than ready to assist at its re-erection, and the poorest man in the village, the hardest-worked, will spare some fraction of his time to help in the re-building. If a new-comer appear in a Korean village, the inhabitants go to work to help him build, or, if necessary, build for him a where-to-lay-his-head.

Such are a few of the characteristics, the most vivid characteristics, I think, of the architecture of Chosön,—an architecture which is even more significant than architecture usually is. Korean architecture is significant of Korean artisticness. It is significant of Korean good sense; for the architecture of Chosön is invariably well-adapted to the climate of the peninsula. But far beyond this, Korean architecture is significant of the Korean love of seclusion, and of the Korean faith in the efficacy of appearances. The Koreans, more perhaps than any other people, realize that fine feathers make fine birds, and the most studied, the most elaborated, and architecturally the most important part of a Korean house is its fence; which of course is not a part of the house at all. This fence may be a hedge, it may be a wall encircling the domains of a magistrate, or engirdling the city. It may be a series of hedges, of moats, of walls, and of gates. The Koreans are exclusive and seclusive to a degree. This should command for them the sympathy of English people. All Koreans strive heroically to put their best feet forward, personally, financially, and architecturally. This should command them the sympathy of Americans. The Korean farmer screens his house inside a quadrangle of hedges, hedges as sweet as are the hedges of North Wales in the month of July. A Korean king hides his palace behind an externity of many walls that are splendid in height, in colour, in detail, in outline, and in material. Walls between which a score of flowers fight each other for the glory of killing every inch of the grass,—walls between which marble-outlined ponds sleep cosily beneath their green and pink and white coverlets of lilies, and of lotus. And the Koreans who are neither princes nor peasants, but who stand between the two, spend a world of thought, and a good deal of money upon the fences—floral or stone—thrown about their homes. Only the poorest of Korean houses —of which there are many—and only the shops— of which there are few—lack some sort of a wall, some manner of a barrier between the private family life, and the public life of the going and coming community.

Korean walls (I mean the walls of masonry which mark the boundaries of a city or the limits of a gentleman's grounds, and not the paper walls of a Korean house) are, without exception,

Chinese in character. But even more important than these walls are the gateways with which they are broken, and above all, the gateways or gates that stand some distance outside the walls. In Far Asia gates have a significance which they never have had, even in our own old Norman days, and never can have, in Europe. Gates are the architectural ceremonies of the East. They frame many of the most ceremonial ceremonies of the East, and it necessarily follows that they are big and georgeous. For never did a picture justify more lavish framing than does the picture of Eastern ceremony. There are three great classes of gates in the Far East: the torii of Japan, the red-arrow gates of Korea, and the pailow of China. But before I try to say something of these three gates, there are two or three pleasant things to be said of the gates that ordinarily pierce the wall of a Korean city. The gates themselves are heavily built of wood, are elaborately ornamented with metal, and slowly swing in a rusty sort of way at sunrise, and at sunset—swing at sunrise to let the people of the city out, and the people of the country in; swing at sunset to let the people of the country out, and the people of the city in. Korea not being a land of machinery, it becomes necessary for a certain number of officials to tend these gates. They are not called gate-keepers, but are officers, rather important officers, if I remember, of the Korean army. Now, an army officer, all the world over, does not mind where he lies, what he eats, or how he suffers—when he is on active service: but when debarred from fighting, the soldier, all the world over, and especially the officer-soldier, wants to be well-housed, well-roomed, well-fed, and above all, well-amused. This seems to be the one military trait which Korea has not yet forgotten. Above the gates that open into Söul, and into every other walled Korean city, are built very cosy little stone houses. In these the soldiers on guard—the gate keepers—play cards, eat rice, munch sweetmeats, and sip arrack. Above the gateways that lead into the houses of Korean magistrates, Korean nobles, and of Korean millionaires, just such houses are built. They are the concert halls of Korea. In them the band of the Korean magistrate, the Korean noble, or the Korean millionaire discourses more or less discordant music, and at delightfully respectful distance from its employer's house. They never play in the cold weather. It has been said that this is so, not because the Korean in whose service they are cares a whit whether their fingers freeze to their instruments or not, but because he is unwilling to open the paper walls of his house wide enough to hear the music that is being played in the gate-houses of his outer walls. I doubt this. A rich Korean, who is covered with layers and layers of silk and wadding, and who sits upon a khan in full fire, and who is surrounded by braziers of charcoal, and whose house is deplorably lacking in ventilation, does not, I think, as a rule, shrink from having his front door or his side wall opened once in a while. Beneath the guard-house building, above the gate of a Korean wall; there can be no khan, for the guard-house is above the gate, and many feet from the ground in which the Khan must be embedded. And so I put it down to the humanity of the average well-to-do Korean that he never makes his band play, on his walls, save in fairly warm weather.

These rooms, these little houses built above the gates of a Korean walled city or the gates of a great man's domain, have been in years past the scenes of many a Korean romance, and even now they are often the favourite retreats or lounging places of Korean poets and philosophers. They are usually furnished with considerable comfort. They are cosy in the autumn and in the spring, and delightfully cool in the summer. They're well above the city's sights, and high above any unpleasant intrusion of the city's sounds, and so are fit resting-places for one who wants to meditate or dream or write poetry, or be at rest, or escape from the hundred nagging vexations of daily life.

Korean walls are adjuncts to Korean gates, and not, as with us, the gates adjuncts to the walls. The walls are built to emphasize the importance of the gates, to supplement them, and to attract attention to them. To the Korean mind the walls are so much less important than the gates that the gates are often built and the walls omitted altogether. Such gates are the torii of Japan, the pailow of China, and the red-arrow gates of Chosön. Every Korean gate has a name, a name that is meant to be impressive and poetical, symbolical of beauty and of good. And doubtless these names are so to Korean ears, but they are apt to strike the European mind of average stolidity as amusing or silly. In Korea, indeed, every edifice of any pretension has a name. The people of the Far East personify their buildings to a great extent, and endue them with individuality, and with human attributes. Royal gateways are often flanked by two immense Chinese lions, or, as they are more generally called, Korean dogs. These dogs are but one of the many most universal expressions of Korean art. They are the one expression of Korean art with which we, in Europe, are very familiar.

There is nothing else in picturesque Korea so picturesque as the red-arrow gates. I wish I might devote a chapter to them, and I am rather appalled at undertaking to at all clearly describe them in a few paragraphs. A dozen or more of the most eminent European authorities on Korea unanimously declare the red-arrow gates to have either been copied from, or to have been the originals of the Japanese torii. Why, in the bulk of literature that has been written about these strange gates of the Far East, little or no mention has been made of the Chinese pailow puzzles me. There can, I think, be no doubt that the three gates are three generations of one architectural family, or that they have had a common origin. The pailow of China are memorial arches, erected, as a rule, to commemorate the virtue and the character of women who have slaughtered themselves that they might follow their husbands to the grave. These arches are heavier than the Japanese torii, or the Korean red-arrow gates, but they are like both in their general outlines and in situation. And all Chinese architecture is very much heavier than the architecture of Korea or of Japan. The torii of Japan marks the approach to a temple, or to some sacred place. It is formed of two upright columns or pillars which lean slightly toward each other at the top, and are crossed by two or three graceful bars ; the upper of which is slightly, but very beautifully curved. The word "torii" is most usually translated " birds' rest," from " tori " a " bird," and " I " " to be," or " rest."   And the theory has been that they were originally built as convenient resting-places for birds : as birds, with all other animals, were sacred in the eyes of the Buddhists.   This translation is unsatisfactory.   The etymology of the word itself, like that of so many other Japanese words, is hidden in a good deal of mystery, and though to-day we find the torii outside of every Buddhist temple in Japan, we also find one outside every Shinto temple in Japan, and it is easily proved that they were first reared outside the Shinto, and not outside the Buddhist temples. Long before Buddhism was introduced into Japan, the torii stood outside numerous Shinto temples. The most plausible translation of the word " torii," though it is not a translation altogether convincing, is " a place of passing through."   It is Mr. Chamberlain, I believe, who gives this translation, but his book is not at my hand, and I am not positive.   Certainly both in Korea and in Japan the birds make a very general resting-place of the torii, and of the red-arrow gates.   But then so do they in China of the pailow, and so do they in America and Europe of the telegraph wires.   It is very possible that from this habit of theirs "torii" has come to mean, or has been thought to mean, "birds' rest." The red-arrow gates of Korea are taller and narrower than the torii of Japan. The red-arrow gate never stands outside a temple, but outside a palace or some high magistracy, and it denotes the approach to a house of the king, or to the house of one of almost kingly authority. So in Söul we find a red-arrow gate standing outside the yamun of the Chinese Resident, one of the many silent, but clearly legible proofs that Korea has long regarded herself as a vassal of China. These gates are painted a most brilliant red, which is the Korean royal colour. The upright columns of a red-arrow gate are crossed by two horizontal bars. These bars are quite straight, and unlike the cross-bars of the torii, the upper one does not extend quite to the top of the perpendicular column. These gates are called arrow-gates because of twenty or more speared-shaped bits of wood that are embedded in the lower of the two horizontal bars, pierce through the upper bar, and extend a little higher than the shaped ends of the perpendicular columns. They are simplicity itself, these red-arrow gates, except for their gorgeous colouring, and altogether lack the elaboration of the Japanese torii. They are thirty feet high at least, often much higher. But however simple in themselves they make wonderful frames for wonderful bits of Korean landscape. On the exact centre of the upper cross-bar rests a peculiar design which represents the positive and negative essences—the male and female essences of Chinese philosophy. This again is surmounted by tongue-shaped or flame-shaped bits of wood, which are supposed to, in some way, represent the power of the king. The two symbols together signify Korea's king as omnipotent, since he is under the protection of China, and has espoused the religion of Confucius. It is noticeable that the torii of Japan invariably marks the vicinity of a temple, or of some building, or some place sacred to one or more of the Japanese deities; while in Korea the red-arrow gate invariably signifies the proximity of the dwelling of temporal power. I am inclined to think that the Koreans borrowed the idea of their red-arrow gates from the Chinese, and that the Japanese seeing them, translated them into torii. If this is so, it is presumable that in both instances the borrowers erected the gates in front of what was to them the most important places in their own countries. The Emperor of Japan is the nominal head of the Shinto religion. In the days when the torii was introduced into Japan, religion was probably a great force in the three islands, and the temples seemed to the Japanese the most appropriate places to be honoured by this arched sign of importance. In Korea, on the other hand, religion is, and for many years has been, under a social and governmental ban. In Korea the king is all, and the gods are naught, so—as a matter of course—the red gates reared their graceful, arrow-crowned heads outside the house of a king, or of a deputed representative of the Chinese emperor.

The bridges of Korea, the big bell at Söul, and a dozen other characteristic details of Korea's rich architecture, all rise up before me and seem to reproach me for passing them by without a word. To touch upon them with anything approaching adequacy would require pages and not words, and the pages at my disposal are growing few. But I can heartily recommend their study and the study of Korean architecture in general to all who are interested in the East, and in architecture, and who are fascinated by the quaint and the symbolical.

CHAPTER VIII.

HOW THE CHINESE, THE JAPANESE, AND THE KOREANS AMUSE THEMSELVES.

THERE is nothing else, I think, that so positively proves the intimate relationship of China, Japan, and Korea, as does the great similarity between their games and their amusements—a similarity which almost amounts to identicalness. If it is true that "*in vino veritas*," it must be equally true that men are most natural when they are happiest, freest from care, and have neither business nor duties beyond recreating themselves. So when we study the Chinese, the Japanese, and the Koreans at play, and find that they all play very much alike, appreciate the same or kindred amusements, have the same methods of feasting, of resting, and of enjoyment, we are justified in concluding that these three peoples are very near of kin. But if they be children of the same parents, they are not the children of one birth, and this to me, at least, is proved by the few but sharp differences between each of their three ways of amusing themselves.

China, Korea, and Japan! And the greatest of these is China. Let us watch them, beginning with China, at their recreations, and then let us note how in those recreations they differ.

Feasts naturally form an important part of the happiness of a people, the majority of whom commonly go hungry. A Chinese dinner is in more than one way startling—to the average European mind. But it is a very good dinner for all that.

I have been at many a Chinese dinner. Sometimes I have sat with the quaint Chinese women, behind the shelter of the lattice. Sometimes I have feasted brazenly with the men; and more than once the women of a Chinese household have, out of courtesy to me, come forth from the prized seclusion of their lattice-screened coign of vantage, and joined me in eating with the commoner faction of the family herd; in breaking bread with men.

Chinese festivals! The subject is so intricate and so interesting that I have not the impertinence to dismiss it in a sentence. But, in passing, I may say that no people enjoy festivals more, no people indulge in them more discreetly, less frequently than do the Chinese.

Chinese ceremonials! Funerals, weddings, and a hundred others! I know, in all the East, nothing more incomprehensible to the average, well educated European mind; nothing more philosophically pregnant to minds that are exceptionally industrious and exceptionally open.

Chinese recreations are almost myriad. They fly kites; they let go perfumed, brightly-lit balloons of silk and of silk-like paper; they light their fire-fly-lit land with a hundred thousand lanterns, and in honour of those lanterns, in indulgence of themselves, they hold a feast.

The dramatic is the chief of all arts. In China dramatic performances take the precedence of all entertainments. A Chinese theatre, at the best, is a barn-like place. It is devoid of scenery. Only men take part in Chinese theatrical performances.

In China, actors are looked down upon as social pariahs, and their sons may not enter for the competitive examinations which are the birthright of almost every Chinaman.

But nevertheless the Chinese have a god of play-acting, and they pay him no small homage. Indeed, all the Chinese deities are supposed to be great theatre-goers; and for their benefit theatrical performances are frequently held in the courtyards of the temples. The people (who have a free *entrée*) flock to these performances and enjoy them as much or even more than the gods are supposed to do.

To almost no Chinese dramatic performance is admission charged. A number of people club together, hire the actors, engage the musicians, put up a shed—on the street, in a field, anywhere, anyhow—invite the entire community—which needs no urging—and the performance begins. Or a rich man is the momentary impresario. But even then the people expect to be admitted, and usually are.

The Emperor of China is a great devotee of the drama. He often commands a play at eight in the morning. Indeed, the day is the more usual hour for all theatrical performances in China.

But the most well worth seeing of Chinese Thespian entertainments are those that take place in the temple courtyards. No need of scenery there! Behind the bamboo stage rise the not unimpressive walls of the queerly-architectured Chinese temple. Where we are wont to have glaring footlights there is a soft, rosy glow, for there great rhododendrons lift their proud and heavy heads. The courtyard is partly surrounded by a wall so old and broken that it might be the veritable old wall of China. From its sides lean double-flowering apricots and the sweet yu-lan, with its thousand blooms of pale peach colour. From the wall's top strange Chinese grasses nod and flower-heavy vines hang. Among the vines and grasses primroses nestle cosily. Beside the wall tulips flaunt, and great clumps of mignonette grow among the hibiscus flowers. The actors are very fine with their crowns of tinsel and their robes of silk. The audience, too, is well worth watching, with their intelligent yellow faces, and their glittering black eyes. They are tense with interest, those Mongolian play-goers. And the Chinese orchestra! Ah! that is droll indeed.

We are apt to think of Chinese music as being noise pure and simple. Certainly very much Chinese music is superlatively noisy. But even Chinese music has its softer side, its refined moments. I remember a little band in Canton that used to make very pleasant lullaby music, and to handle their odd instruments with most considerable taste.

When Noah was learning something of boat-building, the Chinese were, in their Chinese way, expert musicians. Their principal instrument was made of twelve tubes of bamboo. Six tubes were for the sharps, and six for the flats.

To-day the Chinese have over fifty musical instruments—instruments made of stone, of metal, and of wood.

Chinese dramatic literature is unusually interesting. To study it is no mean mental tonic, and it is, I believe, the best way to study the Chinese people, unless one can live among them with some little intimacy.

But I must not linger too long by the wayside of my pleasant subject. Yet I must touch—if only with a sentence—upon four or five of the many other ways in which the Chinese recuperate their overburdened bodies and their jaded minds.

. They take great joy in Nature. Picnics are a most Chinese institution. They are invariably planned to be at some spot where there is an exceptional view. And the picnic party will sit for hours, and watch the hills, or masses of fruit trees in bloom, or the sunset—sit silently too ; for the Chinese, though the noisiest nation on earth, are apt to be hushed in the presence of nature, however much they chatter in the presence of their gods.

The Chinese are intensely fond of gardening. Every Chinaman that can afford it has a flower garden, and in nothing, save the graves of his ancestors, does he take more pride. In the garden's centre there will be a lake—a very round, funny lake—and on its rippleless bosom great drowsy lien-hoas will sleep away their perfumed lives.

The lien-hoa is the Chinese water-lily. There are many varieties. They are single and double. They are red, they are rose, they are white. And some are of an indescribably lovely pale red, delicately streaked with white.

In almost every Chinese garden you will find a summer-house, its roof heavy with festoons of the wisteria. And there will be a pansy bed, a bosque of bamboo, a grove of camellias, a field of chrysanthemums, a world of peonies, trees of peaches, of plums, and of apricots, parallelograms planted with hydrangeas, and clumps of azaleas.

There are two other Chinese pleasures that I must at least mention—opium-smoking and gambling. Both are ineradicable characteristics of the Chinese.

The poppy gives the Chinese masses inestimable alleviation, and does them, I believe, the veriest minimum of harm.

Gambling, I fear, has a more baneful effect upon them. But it is their most positive and commonest diversion, and it will, I fancy, always be their national habit.

I have spoken of Chinese amusements, and now my trouble begins. I am at an entire loss to know how to speak of Korean amusements without repeating myself almost word for word.

I can think of but two Chinese amusements which are not as general in Chosön as in Cathay —card-playing and theatre-going. In Korea it is not good form to play cards, and they are not played openly, except by the soldiers, and the lowest grades of society. Soldiers are allowed to play cards as much as they like, and for a very quaint reason. A soldier is often called upon for night duty. Now after eating, the thing dearest to the average Korean is sleeping, and the Korean government, which is not, from the Far Asiatic point of view, so merciless after all, has decreed that, as the playing of games of chance is more likely than any other thing to keep a man from being sleepy, the Korean soldiers may indulge in any and every game of chance, including those that are played with cards.

Korea is not without theatrical performances, no Eastern land is ; but the theatrical performances of Korea are very different from the theatrical performances of China and of Japan. Indeed, in no branch of amusements do the three countries so differ as they do in the branch dramatic. With the possible exception of the Hindoo and the Mohammedan, the Japanese dramatic school approaches our own more than that of any other Oriental country. I have seen performances in Yeddo that seemed to me to quite merit classification with London productions at the Lyceum, and at the Savoy. Chinese dramatic art is a thing apart, and a law unto itself. It makes little or no appeal to European intelligence, or to European imagination. It is for the Chinese, and takes as little concern as the Chinese themselves voluntarily do of other peoples.

Korean dramatic art, if it is at all akin with the dramatic art of Europe, approaches most nearly the art methods of the high-class music halls, and the best French variety theatres. Every Korean actor is a star, superior to, indifferent to, and independent of scenery.

More often than not, the Korean actor is not only the star, but the entire company. He plays everything—old men, juveniles, low comedians and high tragedians, leading ladies, *ingénueux*, and rough soubrettes—plays them with little or no change of costume, plays them in quick succession, and wholly without aid of scenery. And very clever, indeed, he is to do it. Closely allied as all the three great peoples of the far Orient are in their amusements, the amusements of the Koreans resemble the amusements of China very much more than they do the amusements of Japan; and yet Korean acting is very much more like Japanese than like Chinese acting. This is especially worthy of note, I think, because in every nation in the world, the theatrical is the highest form of amusement.

Korean acting would come, perhaps, more properly under the heading of Korean art than under the head of Korean amusements, or quite as appropriately, perhaps, under the head of Korean religion. For in Korea, as in every other country, acting is not only an exquisite, and one of the highest expressions of a nation's intellectuality, but is the child, almost the first-born child, of that country's religion. It is, perhaps, because Korea has ceased to have a religion that Korea has no theatre, at least, no permanent theatre. The Korean actor gives his performance on the bare paper floor of some rich man's banqueting hall, or at the street corner. The actors of Japan are surrounded with every possible accessory, and with the perfection of accessories. The most faultless stage setting I ever saw, the utmost nicety of properties that I ever saw, and the best trained supers I ever saw, I saw on the stage of a Tokio theatre. The Korean actor has no stage setting, he has no properties, and he never heard of supernumeraries. His theatre—for, after all, I am inclined to withdraw what I said, and to maintain that wherever an artist acts there is a theatre—his theatre consists of a mat beneath his feet, and a mat over his head, and four perpendicular poles separating the two mats. And yet the Korean actor shares very largely the polish, the definiteness of method, and the convincing artisticness of the Japanese actor. If religion had flourished in Korea as it has flourished in Japan, it is probable that, under the sheltering patronage of religion, Korean acting would now equal, if not excel, the best acting of Japan. As it is, the Korean actor is remarkable for his versatility, for his mastery of his own voice, his mastery of facial expression, and his comprehension of, and his reproducing of, every human emotion. A Korean actor will often give an uninterrupted performance of some hours length. He will recite page after page of vivid Korean history; he will chant folk-songs; he will repeat old legends and romances, and he will give Punch and Judy-like exhibitions of connubial infelicity and of all the other ills that Korean flesh is heir to. And he will intersperse this dramatic kaleidoscope with orchestral music of his own producing. Perhaps he has pitched his theatre of mats in the full heat of the noon-day sun, but even so, he only pauses to take big, quick drinks of peppery water, or of a very light, rice wine, in which good-sized lumps of hot ginger float. If the actor is performing at a feast of some mandarin or other wealthy Korean, he is, of course, paid by an individual employer ; and the audience which has, in all probability, been amply dined and amply wined, sit near him, sit at their ease, and in an irregular semicircle. If the performance is given in the street, it is purely a speculation on the part of the actor. The audience sit about on queer little wooden benches, or squat on mats, or stand. And when the actor knows (and this is something which an actor always does know, the acting-world over) that he has struck the high-water mark of his momentary possible histrionic ability, he pauses abruptly and collects such cash as his audience can or will spare. The result is usually very gratifying to the actor. The audience want to see the play out, and the player won't play on until he is paid. A street audience appreciates the play highly, appreciates it none the less, perhaps, because it—the audience—eats and drinks from the first scene until the last. It is an interesting sight to see in front of the temporary temple of a Korean actor a concourse of men with eyes a-stark with pleasure, and faces a-bulge with refreshment, but it is a sight which is not too open to the criticism of the people in whose own theatres ices and coffees and sweetmeats are hawked about between the acts. It always seems to me that we insult art grossly when we tacitly admit that we cannot sit through a fine dramatic performance without the stimulant of meat or of drink. The Japanese also eat between the acts, but then they have the excuse of sitting through performances that are sometimes twelve hours long. We lack that excuse in Europe. And though the Koreans munch and sip through the intensest moments of a Korean theatrical exhibition, no dramatic performance in Korea lasts, unless I mistake, for more than three, or at the utmost, four hours. A Korean actor, to attain to any eminence in his profession, must be able to improvise, and probably in no Eastern country, certainly in no Western country, is the art of improvising carried to so high a degree of perfection as it is in Korea. The Korean actor also approaches somewhat to the Anglo-Saxon clown. He must be quick with cheap witticisms, glib jests, and jokes that would be coarse if they were not above all stupid. He must be ready with topical quips, for the Korean crowd will have its laugh, or it won't pay. This branch of his trade he is seldom called upon to ply when he performs at private entertainments.

The Chinese, the Japanese, and the Koreans are all inveterate picnickers. They are all intensely fond of Nature, and of feasting out of doors. All three of these peoples take the greatest delight in tobacco. Opium is smoked in Korea more than in Japan, but far less than in China. But all the Koreans, whatever their age, whatever their station, whatever their sex, smoke tobacco almost as perpetually as do the Burmese. The Koreans use a pipe, of which the bowl is so small that it only holds a pinch or two of tobacco, and the stem of which is so long that it is almost impossible to light one's own pipe. When not in use, a gentleman's pipe is carried in his sleeve, or tucked into his girdle. The labouring man or the coolie usually thrusts his down his neck between his coat and his back. All three of these peoples are great patrons of professional story-tellers, and of magicians. The Japanese excel the others in magic, and the Koreans excel in story-telling.

It is a favourite pastime both in Japan and Korea to watch trained dancers. There is no dancing in China.

In Korea fights are the occasions of great national joy. In Japan skilful wrestlers and fencers give really artistic exhibitions, but never carry them to the point of brutality. But in Korea a fight is a real fight. Blow follows blow; limbs are bruised, dislocated, and broken. During the first month of the year it is legal, and is the height of Korean good form, to indulge in as many fights as possible. Antagonistic guilds, numbering hundreds of men, face each other at some convenient and appointed spot, and in the sight of thousands of enthusiastic spectators, fight out an entire year's debt of envy and hatred. Men engage in the roughest of personal combat; men who during the other eleven months of the year scarcely fight upon the gravest provocation. A considerable fight between two Korean women of the poorest class is not unknown, and some of them fight extremely well. Mothers often devote considerable time training their small sons in the art of defence, and of fisty attack. Every Korean town, almost every Korean village, has a champion fighter. Prize-fights are to Korea what the race-course is to Europe and to Anglo-Asia. The spectators bet until they have nothing left to bet with, and then very often start an amateur fight of their own. Korean gentlemen do not as a rule fight, nor are they apt to attend a public fight. They often, however, go to very great expense in engaging professionals to give private exhibitions of their prowess. There is one rather comical side to a Korean fight. Every Korean wears an abundance of big clothing, and the antagonists never dream of disrobing in the least. And so two fighting Koreans, from a little distance, look as much like two fighting feather beds as anything else. Debt is said to be the cause of nine out of ten of the fights that are not exhibitions of skill. In Korea, as in China, it is a great disgrace not to pay all your debts on, or before the New Year; and any Korean who fails to do so is very apt to find himself involved in a pugilistic reckoning. Club fights and stone fights are very common. When a stone fight is proposed the friends or admirers of the combatants spend some hours in collecting two mounds of small rough stones. Then the battle begins, and it is a battle. Sometimes it is a duel, and sometimes fifty or even a hundred take an active part in it, pelting each other as rapidly and as roughly as possible.

But the most important, and the most popular of all amusements in Korea is that of eating and drinking. Intemperance, I fear, is very common, and is so little condemned by public opinion that it is quite as much a national recreation as a national vice, but it is seldom or never indulged in by women, and even the geisha girls are sobriety itself. The Koreans drink everything and anything of an intoxicating kind that they can get. They are improving, however, in this respect, of late years. Japanese beer is somewhat displacing the heavier rice liquors, and among the very wealthiest people both claret and champagne are popular. But the Koreans eat as much as ever they did, and no other people extract so much genuine enjoyment from eating. The Koreans season their food more highly, and use more chillies, more mustard than any other people in Asia. They are very fond of the taro, a smooth, small, sweet potato. They devour sea-weed by the pound, and eat lily-bulbs by the bushel. Here is the *ménu* of a very elegant Korean dinner :—

Boiled pork with rice wine.
Macaroni soup.
Chicken with millet wine.
Boiled eggs.
Pastry.
Flour.
Sesame and honey pudding.
Dried persimmons and roasted rice with honey.

Both the Koreans and the Chinese, at least those who can afford it, use very much more meat than do the Japanese.

Sleeping is another great national amusement in Korea. I know no other people that seem to take so much positive enjoyment in sleep, and who go at it so deliberately and systematically. They positively regard it as a pastime.

The Koreans are fond of music, and have many concerts, but then so, too, do the Japanese and the Chinese. Fishing is a popular sport in all three countries.

The Koreans have many festivals, at which they indulge themselves in as much pleasure as possible. As in China, New Year's day is perhaps the most important, and certainly the most generally observed of the festivals. The Korean New Year customs and the Chinese New Year customs are almost identical. I won't describe the New Year customs of Korea, because to do so, I should have to say almost word for word what I recently wrote about the Chinese New Year. Kite-flying and top-spinning occupy a good deal of the time of old and young in China, in Korea, and in Japan. Kite fights and top battles are of very frequent occurrence, and are really very pretty to watch.

The Koreans are very fond of visiting, and of being visited, but in this again, they in no way differ from the other peoples of the further Orient.

Besides fishing, there are three manly sports in vogue in Korea, and I believe, three only; all others being considered undignified and ungentlemanly. The three are archery, falconry, and hunting. Indeed, I scarcely know if I am right in including hunting in the list. It is so very generally pursued as a business, and not as a pleasure. I believe that a few Koreans do sometimes hunt for sport, and very good sport they usually get. Deer, tigers, leopards, badgers, bears, martens, otters, sables, wolves, and foxes are abundant, and the peninsula is full of feathered life. Pheasants are as plentiful, as beautiful, and as toothsome in Korea as they are in China. And they have wild geese, plover, snipe, varieties of ducks, teal, water hens, turkeys and turkey-bustards, herons, eagles, and cranes ; and the woods are full of hares and of foxes.

Archery is considered in Korea the most distinguished of recreations. Every Korean gentleman, from the king down, is, or tries very hard to be, expert at archery. They use a tight, short bow, never over three feet long, and arrows of bamboo. The Koreans are wonderful marksmen, and professional archers are among the most popular of public entertainers.

Falconry is almost as popular as archery, and every nobleman has at least one falcon. The falcon is invariably extensively and gaudily ward-robed, and has usually a personal attendant. Falcon competitions, both public and private, are frequent, and among the nobility are often made the occasion of elaborate entertainments.

The Koreans have a quaint little festival, called " Crossing the Bridges." Söul abounds in queer little stone bridges. A moonlight night is chosen for the festival. Usually a man and a woman walk to the centre of the bridge, and make a wish for the ensuing year, or pray for good-luck, and search the stars for some augury of prosperity. They have a number of peculiar, picturesque customs in connection with " Crossing the

Bridges," but I fancy that with both men and women it is more an excuse for a night out than anything else.

The Koreans are even more impersonal than the Chinese. The Japanese are intensely personal. The Korean is impersonal in business, and impersonal in pleasure. He feasts with other men, and mingles with other men in all his amusements, but his interest is absorbed by his surroundings, and not by his companions. Introspection, and the study of other men, are seldom or never methods of Korean self-entertainment. Nature is after all the greatest entertainer of the Koreans; and to study Nature, to watch her, and to fall more and more deeply in love with her, is a Korean's greatest amusement.

CHAPTER IX.

A GLANCE AT KOREAN ART.

" Far Eastern art draws its inspiration from Nature, not from man. It thus stands, in the objects of its endeavour, in striking contrast to what has ever been the main admiration and study of our own, the human figure. A flower, a face—matter as it affects mind, mind as it affects matter—from such opposite sources spring the two Art, or the desire to perpetuate and reproduce the emotions, must, of course, depend upon the character of those emotions. Now to a Far Oriental Nature is more suggestive and man less so than with us."—PERCIVAL LOWELL.

THE subject of Korean art is vast, intricate, and difficult. It could not possibly be covered, even in the most superficial way, in one chapter, or in a series of several chapters. But it would be preposterous to altogether exclude it from any book whose pages are devoted to Korea generally. For perhaps the most really interesting thing about Korea, and certainly one of the most interesting things to be said about Korea is this :— Korea was the birthplace of a great deal that is finest and highest in the art of that wonderful art country—Japan.

P

A great deal that is most distinguished in Korean art, past and present, is undeniably indigenous to Korea, but, on the other hand, the Korean artists have borrowed or absorbed a good deal from the arts of other countries. In the early days of its prosperity Korean art seems to have owed a great deal to China. But, even in its infancy, through the long years of its magnificent splendour, and in these days of its decay or of trance, Korean art always has had, and has, a marked individuality, and bears the indubitable hall-mark of genuine originality.

In the beginning, then, Korean art was probably a mingling of the national expression of an intensely artistic people, and what was most striking in the rich, but less graceful art of China. Under the Sung dynasty, between the years 960 and 1333 A.D., lay the most brilliant period of China's literary existence, and perhaps the most brilliant period of her art life. And it was also between these years that Korean art reached, and for some time maintained, its highest perfection.

No careful art student who visits both countries, or has access to typical collections of the art productions of both countries, can fail to observe that apparently either Persia has distinctly influenced the art of Korea, or Persia's art been distinctly influenced by Korea. Probably both are true. Persian embassies and Korean embassies were wont to meet in Pekin. Very probably showed each other the presents sent by their respective masters to the Chinese Emperor. These presents were always largely made up of works of art. And their inspection probably led to an interchange of presents between the embassies themselves, and later on, to reciprocal studies, between Persia and Korea, of the art methods of the two countries. Korea has excelled in fret-work, in scroll-work, and in a great variety of arabesque decorations, and in all of these has very largely followed Persian lines.

The key-note of Korean art, as the key-note of all Far Eastern and, indeed, of most Oriental art, is the inferior place held in it by the study of the human figure. Far Eastern art is a study of nature and of decorations. This is even more true of Korea than of China or Japan, though the Koreans excel both the Chinese and the Japanese in their drawing of animals. The chief characteristic of Korean decorative art is its chastity. One cannot fail to be reminded by it of the severe simplicity of old Grecian art. A good specimen of Korean pottery or porcelain is never heavily covered with decoration. A Korean vase, or a Korean bowl, is simple and elegant of outline, and the surface is finely finished, but probably three-fourths of that entire surface is undecorated. The old specimens of Japanese Satsuma (the Koreans taught the Japanese how to make Satsuma) are usually distinguishable from the new and cheaper, because the former are touched with decoration, and the latter are hidden beneath it. The Koreans use colour very lavishly when they use it at all. But conventional design, conventionalized decorations, and decorations which are more exact copies of nature, whether in black and white or in colour, they use very carefully, and never crowd them together. Their porcelains are not so glazed as those of Japan, and the usual, or favourite colour is a creamy white. The dragon, which is so conspicuous a personage in all Far Eastern art, is perpetually drawn by Korean artists in colour, and by Korean artists in black and white, but is rather sparingly used on the Korean pottery; which in this differs from the potteries of China and Japan. The mythical animals and the symbolical animals, though they all figure largely in Korean art, are not often found on Korean porcelain. The Koreans value highly all sorts of crackle ware, and have been excelled, I fancy, in its manufacture by no other people.

Griffis says: " Decoration is the passion of the Orient, and for this, rather than for creative or ideal art, must we look from this nation, to whose language gender is unknown, and in which personification is unthought of, though all nature is animate with malignant or beneficent presences. Abstract qualities embodied in human form are unknown to the Korean, but his refined taste enjoys whatever thought and labour have made charming to the eye by its suggestion of pleasing images to the imagination. His art is decorative, not creative or ideal. His choice pieces of bric-a-brac may be rougher and coarser than those of Japan, but their individuality is as strongly marked as that of the Chinese, while the taste displayed is severer than that of the later Japanese."

Perhaps the design that they most often employ, in their decorative art, is the well-known "wave-pattern." We find it on their porcelain, on their bronzes, in the most conventional of their pictures, and even on their coins. Some one has suggested that it is perhaps used on the small copper coins to symbolize their circulation and fluctuation in value. The wave-pattern symbolizes successive and interminable wave-motion. The love of the Korean artist for water in nature, and for conventionalized water effects in decoration, amounts to a passion. Water in some form or phase is introduced into almost every Korean picture, and on to the majority of the porcelains, bronzes, the lacquers, and into the carvings. We find the wave-pattern beautifully executed on curtains and panels, on armour and on weapons. It often circles the columns of a building, and is conspicuous in interior architectural decorations. A strand of twisting, turning, curling waves is commonly the handle of a fine Korean teapot, and many a Korean dish, or vase, or bowl rests upon a porcelain or bronze bed of seemingly angry waves. The Japanese have seized upon the wave-pattern, and have vastly improved it. It is doubtless through their much exported, and much copied wares that we have become very familiar with it; and I have not infrequently seen it mingled with incongruous European patterns, in fancy printing, both in London, on the Continent, and in America—used for the background of decorative initial letters, or introduced into fancy tail-pieces.

The chrysanthemum was the favourite, the most favoured, and the most studied flower in Korea long before it became the imperial flower, the badge of Japan. The Koreans have always been, and are, wonderfully skilled in rearing it; and in reproducing it in colour, in black and white, in relief, and in conventional designs. We find it whenever we turn our eyes toward Korean objects of art. We find it, or some design suggestive of it, in Korean brocades, and in Korean carvings, and many of the most beautiful Korean borders have been designed from ingenious arrangements of its petals. In several ways the chrysanthemum lends itself with peculiar facility to Korean art ideals. It is rich, splendid, and varied in colour, and the Koreans have a passion for colour. It is interesting and noble in shape, and comes out splendidly in relief, or in half-relief. It is beautiful, but unique, and sometimes even grotesque in outline, and all the Eastern peoples admire the grotesque. Certainly the artists of Korea and of Japan understand the grotesque's usefulness in art above all other artists, and employ it to relieve gentler, simpler forms of beauty, which might grow monotonous if used perpetually. Clouds and stars and the sun are utilized in a variety of ways by the Korean decorative artist. And a conventional pattern, called " the dragon's tooth," is extremely striking, and is nicely adaptable to vases or dishes that are big at the base, and small at the top.

Lacquer has been for centuries as commonly used in Korea as in Japan, but it has never reached the perfection, the artisticness in the former country that it has in the latter.

Korea was once the store-house of innumerable and invaluable works of art ; art treasures of great variety, fine in design, excellent in execution, and rich in symbolism. To-day there are comparatively few art treasures in Korea. The nobles and the rich men probably each have a few hidden away. The king has a number. And some are still to be found in the ostracized monasteries, in the nunneries, and in other unexpected places. But Chosön is no longer the great art treasure-house she once was. In the palaces and the temples of China and Japan are to be seen many of what were once Korea's most prized works of art. And these have been taken as booty from Korea, or sent by Korea as tribute. But the peninsula has not continued in her old glory of art production. Korean art has deteriorated in quality, and in many of its branches shrunk to something nominal in quantity, because great bodies of her best artists and artisans have been sent to Japan, or have gone there. Keenly alive to all that is beautiful in nature, and all that is most exquisite in art, the Japanese readily appreciated the high degree of excellence that had been attained by the artists of Chosön. Not content with taking to Japan the most perfect specimens of Korean art, the Japanese offered every inducement to the best Korean artists to settle in Japan, and spread throughout Japan their superior knowledge of art, and skill in art work. To the instructions of the Koreans the Japanese

owed their unrivalled skill in making the beautiful
Satsuma faïence, and the almost as beautiful
Imari porcelain. The Koreans taught the
Japanese how to carve wood, and then, apparently,
forgot how to do it themselves; though there are
still in Korea some very beautiful specimens of
fine carving, especially in the royal palace at Söul.
The majority of Japanese patterns for brocades
and for stuffs, and many of their favourite designs
for embroidery, are purely and indisputably
Korean.

A scholar, who seems to me always anxious to
do Japan full justice, has written :—

"The existence of any special traits or
principles of decoration, or a peculiar set of
symbols in Korean art, has been thus far hardly
known. When fully studied these will greatly
modify our ideas of Oriental art, and especially
of the originality of the Japanese designers.
Korea was not only the road by which the art
of China reached Japan, but it is the original
home of many of the art-ideas which the world
believes to be purely Japanese."

The Japanese themselves, to be fair to them,
do not claim to have a largely original art, and
my attention was first called to the magnitude of
Japan's art debt to Korea by a Japanese gentleman in Tokio.

Old Persian writers express the greatest admiration for Korean porcelains, and for the beautiful decorated saddles that were sent to Persia from Chosön. The Koreans still excel in the making of gorgeous and (after once the eyes grow accustomed to their gorgeousness) really beautiful saddles. They are inlaid with pearls, and are richly embroidered. Bows and arms and fans are among the many things that the Koreans used to, and still do, make. They are beautiful with pearls, with jade, and with gold and silver and iron inlaying. The Koreans once made splendid and beautiful bells, and were expert in all sorts of metal work, but they have lost or laid aside these arts to a very great extent. There are still some very fine bells in the peninsula, and some beautiful Korean bells in Japan, but their manufacture dates back a long time. And this is also usually true of many of the best specimens of all kinds of Korean artwork that we find in Chosön or in Japan. It is true of most of the beautiful images found in the temples, and many of the vases, the braziers, the incense-burners, the trenchers, the kettles, the bowls, the decanters, and the censors, all of which are exceedingly graceful in form, pure in outline, and decorated with simplicity and dignity.

The throne in the palace of Söul is a very beautiful example of well-controlled art. It is simplicity itself, but it is as majestic as it is simple; perfect in every detail, royal in its proportions, and in severe but perfect taste.

Among the minor arts that still flourish in Korea is that of toy-making. The Korean toy-makers really are artists, and the playthings of the children of the well-to-do are so carefully designed and so faithfully executed, that in their little way they have every claim to be considered works of art. Armour, palanquins—indeed, all the impedimenta of Korean daily life, and of the daily life of old Korea—are reproduced with minute exactness, and very wonderful toys are made out of bits of tiger skins and of the fur of the tiger and other wild beasts.

The battle-flags and the banners of Korea are interesting both to the student of history and the student of art. The mysticism and the symbolism that is so characteristic of all Korean art is noticeable on almost every Korean flag.

The strange animals that we find in Korean art, animals that are like none that ever lived, are symbolical, and, to the Korean mind, typify a great deal that the Koreans think it important to remember.

A branch of art which is much thought of in

Chinese-Asia, and is there indeed a fine art, is
pen-work or brush-work.   In this art the Koreans
are as adept to-day as they ever have been—as
adept as the Chinese or the Japanese.   Fine
specimens of caligraphy are written with a brush
—written upon scrolls of silk or of soft paper,
and are either put away to be treasured, or are
hung upon the walls as ornaments of great interest.   The last time I was in Tokio the wife of
a Japanese official, whose home is very rich in
paintings, both European and Japanese, showed
me, with great pride, her collection of such
scrolls—scrolls, all of which were specimens of
fine writing.   Very much such scrolls form the
principal wall decoration of the study of the
Chinese minister in London, and such scrolls are
among the most cherished household gods of
every well-to-do Korean.   The Koreans write with
the greatest ease and elegance, and it is almost
as natural for them to draw and paint very
fairly well as it is for them to write.

The making of fine pottery is almost, if not
quite, a lost art in Korea, but they still know the
secret of, and still make and use, the exquisite
tints and the matchless colours that characterized
their glazes in the days when Korean art was at
its greatest height.   The Korean potters are
among the nomads of the peninsula.   A family,

or several families, of potters choose some spot where wood and clay are convenient, and there they build their huts, and there they live till the wood or the clay is exhausted. All Korean pottery is fired in ovens that are heated with wood. There are no great potteries in Korea or in Japan. Each specimen of their art is the individual work of an individual, and in this, perhaps, lays one of the secrets of the fascination of any genuine work of art from these countries. The most beautiful piece of porcelain that has ever been made in China, Japan, or in Korea, has probably been made in some humble little hut and fired by an insignificant-looking little oven.

I have spoken elsewhere of the famous Chinese lion, or Korean dog. It is more grotesque than beautiful, and is chiefly interesting because it has so strong a hold upon the affections of three so different peoples. For a conservative Asian, he is a very great traveller, is this Korean dog. He has found his way into every fancy bazaar, and every cheap notion shop in Europe and America; and we really feel quite as if we had met an old friend when we stumble upon him in Yeddo, in Pekin, or in quaint Söul.

It is being constantly urged against Far Eastern art that it is artificial. Mr. Lowell refutes this so clearly, so distinctly, with so much discernment, and to my mind, so convincingly, that I feel it would be a pity to refute it in any other words. He says :—

" Far from being artificial, Far Eastern art is emphatically natural. The reason that it does not so appear to us at first is due to two causes. The first is very simple—an absence with us of what the Far Oriental sees around him at home. A picture of snow-peaks would undoubtedly appear conventional, in the sense used above, to a man who had dwelt all his life on the plains, and never heard of such things as white-headed mountains. The second cause is that certain very salient features of his landscapes have engrossed the Far Oriental attention, to the partial neglect of other less striking but, perhaps, even more common scenes.

" Every traveller knows the effect of this in other things beside art. Narrators insensibly, if not on purpose, pick out the salient points of any land to give an idea of it to those to whom it is an un-discovered country. The result is, that on acquaintance no country seems so odd as imagina-tion, fed on a few startling facts, has pictured it to be ; and yet, for all that, the facts may be per-fectly true. Now, what we do to give others an idea of foreign lands, the Far Oriental does to give himself an idea of his own. His art, by reason of this strong simplicity, is all the higher art."

Landscape gardening holds a prominent place among the arts of Korea, and is as well understood, and as generally practised to-day as it has ever been in the history of the peninsula. Water forms the principal, and the indispensable feature of every Korean garden. Indeed, the pond, which must be in the centre of the garden, often takes up nine-tenths of the garden's entire area. This pond is always called a "lotus pond." Usually the lotus is there, but not always, and its absence only emphasizes the title of the pond. It is interesting to notice how indispensable the sight of water is to the Koreans, and it speaks a great deal, I think, for their genuine love of Nature.

Korea is so surrounded by water, so intersected with rivers, and has so many high hills from which water can be seen for some distance, and down which rivulets and water-falls break, that every Korean must be very familiar with water in all its moods and tenses. But he does not tire of it. On the contrary, a Korean who has his domain on the very sea-shore, will dig up the larger part of his garden for the sake of having an artificial lotus-pond ; that he may sit on the artificial island in its centre and fish and dream and watch the water. Fantastic groups of strange rock work are put in almost every Korean garden: groups to which European eyes have to grow very used before they can see any beauty in them.

Korean music, like almost all Asiatic music, requires a great deal of study before we can at all understand it or like it. Its scale differs entirely from our gamut—differs even more than do Korean instruments from ours. Japanese music is of Korean origin, but has changed greatly of later years. But all classical Japanese music is still identical with Korean music, which has changed little or not at all. Korean government labourers are called to and released from their day's work by music, and to music do the gates of a Korean city close or open for the day.

When Korea was in its infancy she was thrown into intimate contact with China. Korea had not had time to develop a literature, and so she very *naïvely* adopted the literature of China. Chinese literature is the classical literature of Korea still. The great majority of Korean books (and they are not surprisingly many), are written and printed in Chinese. The Koreans have neglected their own language and its literary possibilities for centuries. Still there is considerable poetry written in the Korean tongue (but in the Chinese character almost always), and we may consider the writing of this poetry as one of Korea's national arts.

" Poetry parties " are a popular form of Korean picnics. A number of friends meet at some unusually beautiful spot. They have been preceded by servants carrying writing materials and wine. Very gravely the competitors (for such they are) set to work. They sun and joy themselves in the beauty of the scene, they sip the cup that cheers, but alas! intoxicates too! and when they have enough assimilated the beauty of the scene and the gladness of the wine, then they write verses. The verses take the form of songs, or are ballads in praise of nature. They write of the bamboo, of the stars, of the storm, of moonlight and of sunrise, but never of woman !

CHAPTER X.

KOREA has no religion. This is a sweeping statement, I know, and one that is susceptible of a great deal of dispute, but I believe that in the main it is true. The books that have been written during the last hundred years about Korea teem with thick chapters on Korea's religion, but for all that, I believe that Korea is without religion. There are without doubt Koreans who are deeply and genuinely religious, but they are so infinitesimal a fraction of the population of the peninsula that they no more justify us in crediting Korea with a religion than the handful of Theosophists, who are probably in England to-day, would justify a Korean in crediting England with an at all large acceptance of Theosophy. Buddhism, which was once as dominant in Korea as ever it has been in China or Japan, has been almost destroyed. Confucianism is still a great power in Korea, as it must be in every country where ancestor-worship and the sanctity of the family are the backbone of the nation's moral existence. But I maintain that Confucianism is not, properly speaking, a religion. It is a theory of ethics, a code of morals, admirable, sublime even, but it is not, as I understand the word religion, a religion. There are superstitions in Korea and to spare. The common people are as superstitious as the common people of any other civilized country, which is saying a great deal, and the upper classes are by no means free from superstition. But who shall venture to call superstition a religion? Unless we call superstition and religion synonymous; unless we accept Confucianism as an individual and actual religion; or unless we say that a few scattered monasteries, that must by law be built far beyond the walls of a city—monasteries inhabited by monks, who are looked down upon even by the common people, and are not allowed within the gates of any city; monasteries that are resorted to by the leisure classes for revel and for roystering, and never for prayer or penitence—unless we say that these constitute a national religion, we must, I think, admit that Korea is distinctly irreligious.

The real difficulty in deciding whether Korea is

in any way religious or altogether irreligious lies in the difficulty of distinguishing clearly between religion and superstition. The dividing line between the two is often indistinct—sometimes missing altogether—so perhaps I am wrong in saying that a country so amply dowered with superstition is devoid of religion.

I base my statement that Korea has no religion not upon the absence of religion from Korea, not upon the paucity of religion in Korea, but upon the fact that in Korea religion is neither respected nor respectable. Of course, if we define religion as broadly as do some of the most eminent authorities (Rossiter Johnson, W. Smith, Bishop Taylor, Macaulay, and a host of others), and admit that atheism and superstition are forms of religion—and I am far from sure that they are not —my statement totters, if it does not altogether tumble.

Buddhism was until three hundred years ago strong in Korea, and Confucianism, which, if not a religion, is the most elaborate, and one of the most perfect systems of morality that the world has ever known, and has served humanity better than most religions, is strong in Korea still. A study of these two is, as is the study of all the higher Oriental doctrines, beliefs, and systems of

thought, intensely interesting, and the temptation
to dwell here upon Buddhism and Confucianism is
great. But I fancy that everyone who is interested in reading about so remote a part of the
East as Korea is more or less familiar with the
outlines at least of both Buddhism and Confucianism, and so I will content myself with trying
to tell how the first was driven out of Chosön,
and how the second is still the guardian angel of
such morality as the peninsula possesses.

Buddhism flourished there for centuries, and it
was at least tolerated until the Japanese invasion
in 1592. Indeed, up to that time Korea was not
only not without a religion, but she was not without several. The religions of the Far East are as
easy-going as the peoples—they are modest as a
rule, the beliefs of further Asia—and rub along
together very amicably, no one of them seeming
over-sure that it is better than its fellows.

Three hundred years ago, when two great
Japanese warriors, Konishi and Kato, with their
respective armies landed in Korea, each was so
anxious to have the glory of reaching and
conquering the capital before the other, that
neither dare pause to subdue the towns and the
fortresses (and many of these latter were monasteries) that lay along his route. Yet neither

dare leave behind him a long track of unsubdued and, for those days, well-armed country. In this dilemma they dressed themselves and their followers in the garbs of Buddhist priests, and so by strategy made their entrance into the walled cities, and into the forts, and once in, put the inhabitants, the unprepared soldiers and monks, to death. About thirty years afterwards, when Korea had shaken off, for the time at least, the Japanese yoke, the Korean priests suffered for the cupidity of the Japanese generals ; as the innocent so generally do suffer for the guilty in this nice world of ours. The royal decree went throughout Korea that no Buddhist priest might dwell or even pass within the gates of a walled city. The priests fled to the mountains, and there erected themselves such dwellings as they could. The monasteries, in which they had lived within the city's walls, crumbling away with time, and decaying with disuse, ceased to be architectural features of any Korean city. And this is why all Korean cities are so monotonous in aspect. For religion has been the patron of architecture as of art, of music, of literature, and of drama the world over, and more especially so in the Orient. The priests of the temples of Buddha, having incurred the disfavour of the government, rapidly lost what hold they had had upon the people. And the nation, which had always considered its king almost mightier and more divine than its very gods, soon ceased to pay tribute to, or ask the services of, a body of men who had lost the royal countenance. Then, too, the Koreans are great dwellers in cities. They go far into the country to look at Nature, to rest, and to amuse themselves, but it would never occur to the Korean mind to journey far for prayer or sacrifice. So the revenues of the monasteries fell off. Men well-born and well-to-do ceased to join the order. And little by little Korean Buddhism passed away, until now it is but a wraith of its old self.

This at least is the most general account of how Korea ceased to be Buddhist, but its authenticity is disputed by several of the most reliable historians, and by one, at least, who has written in English. These historians claim that some centuries ago all the powerful people in Korea were divided into two factions—one Buddhist, one Confucist—and great was the rivalry between these two. Social war ensued, and the Buddhists, who had become corrupt and enervated, were terribly defeated. Buddhism was forbidden to dwell within the capital or within the cities. True, the monasteries that had always been important features of the rural landscape were in no way interfered with, but " banishment from the cities produced two results. First, desuetude rendered the mass of the people quite oblivious to religious matters; and secondly, the withdrawal of religion from the seats of power threw the profession into disfavour with the aristocracy. . . . Here, then, we have a community without a religion—for the cities are to a peculiar degree the life of the land—a community in which the morality of Confucius for the upper classes, and the remains of old superstitions for the lower, takes its place."

How, then, in Korea have the religiously mighty fallen! For Buddhist monks once formed a fourth portion of the entire male population of Chosön, and there were tens of thousands of them in Söul alone. At first thought it seems strange that now any Korean should be found willing to embrace the monastic life; but the Koreans are not industrious, many of them are wretchedly poor, and life in the monasteries affords the greatest opportunity for the indolent, dreamy, and meditative life, and the proximity to Nature, which is so dear to the Korean heart. No Korean monk is called upon to do hard manual labour, and it is still almost a religion with the Koreans, rich and poor, to give something toward the sustenance, and even toward the creature comforts of the brothers. So laziness, and poverty, and misery keep the Korean monasteries and the Korean nunneries from falling into utter disuse. Strangely enough, the monks of Korea rarely or never have the brutal sinful-looking faces that characterize so many of their brethren in China.

I should divide the religion, or the irreligion, of Korea into rationalism: the religion of the patricians; and superstition: the religion of the plebeians. Both rationalism and superstition are well controlled by a system of morality which is rooted in Confucianism, and impregnably enwalled by ancestor-worship.

Rationalism and superstition have their points of touch—points at which the one is indistinguishable from the other—lost in the other—in Korea as everywhere else.

I do not mean that reason and unreason ever lose themselves in each other, though, like other rival powers, the boundary line between them may be narrower than any fraction of any hair, and quite imperceptible to human eyes.

Korean rationalism is practically identical with rationalism the world over. Korean superstitions are unique in form if not in essence. It merits at least passing notice that Reason expresses herself in one way everywhere, and that Unreason in different parts of the earth speaks in tongues as differing as fantastic.

The expression of Korean superstition is

picturesque. The more picturesque a superstition is the more impregnable it is.

Korean demon-worship is positively fascinating. Superstition has not always been the power in Korea that it is now. In Korea religion and superstition have played a long game of see-saw. The Koreans outgrew their early superstitions, discarded them, and embraced a highly civilized and civilizing form of religion; then they discarded that religion. Now, the average human mind must believe in something outside of its own material ken, beyond its own demonstrating. *Quod erat demonstrandum* forms no part of the rituals and the creeds of most religions, so when the time came that Buddha and his coterie of well-bred and fairly rational deities had practically been banished from Korea, the Koreans fell back on their old superstitions, and to-day superstition and its ridiculous rites are more rife in Korea than in any other civilized country.

There are three classes of supernatural beings in whom the people of Korea believe—the demons who work all manner of evil, the beneficent spirits whose practice it is to do good occasionally, and who semi-occasionally combat the evil spirits, and an intermediate class of spirits who dwell, as a rule, on the mountains, and neither work good nor evil, but who, in themselves and in their lives, are the subjects of much charming folk-lore. The Korean—the Korean of the populace—the superstitious Korean attributes all his ills to demons. He, being a Korean, cannot conceive that Nature can be malignant, nor can he conceive that he is ever punished for breaking laws of whose very existence he is ignorant. So he peoples the air, the sea, and the rocks with devils of earthquake, devils of pestilence, devils of lightning, devils of hurricane, and a thousand other devils of blight and of sorrow. Having determined that they cause all his troubles, he then sets about doing the best he can to propitiate the spirits of evil. Korean demons are supposed to be very small, and I have never heard of one to whom much physical strength was attributed; and almost always when it comes to a face-to-face contest between one of them and a powerful man (and such contests occur very often in Korean myths), the demon has the worst of it. Still, the majority of the Korean populace live in unceasing terror and dread of these demons. Korean methods of circumventing them are delightful, and delightfully simple. I have already spoken of the beasts that sit on guard on many Korean roofs. They are supposed to be the most efficacious combatants of the Korean devils; but the privilege of having them

is rather monopolized by royalty and by the high
favourites of the royal family. On lintels of
the houses of well-to-do Koreans are usually hung
two oblong pieces of coloured paper upon which
are drawn in black, or two oblong pieces of white
paper on which are drawn in colours, terrible
enough portraits of two famous old generals. One
of these warriors was a Chinaman, the other was
a Korean, and both are renowned in the legends
of the peninsula as having waged highly successful warfare against several evil spirits of Chosön,
and their portraits are supposed to protect the
houses, outside of which they hang, from the invasion of the imps of mischief and of misery.
Korean devils, for some unfathomable reason, are
supposed to be far more powerful indoors than
out, and so the Koreans are at special pains to
exclude their devilships from Korean interiors.
The Korean householder, who is debarred by
poverty or by his own social inferiority both
from using the roof-scarecrows, and from hanging
counterfeit presentments of the two old warriors
on his portals, fastens a strip of cloth and some
wisps of rice straw outside his door. He fastens the
rice straw there in the hope that the devil about
to enter may be hungry, and stop to gorge himself and then go away. He fastens the bit of cloth
(which must be torn from some old garment of

his own), because the Koreans have the nice taste to consider their devils extremely stupid, and so believe that any devil who is confronted with a fragment of a man's garment will mistake it for the man himself, and, in view of how often men have defeated devils, fly and trouble that house no more.

The evil spirits of Korea are also frightened away by noise; noise so enormous, so metallic, so discordant, so altogether diabolical, that it is no wonder the devils rush from it, rush on their wings of sulphurous flame, and the only wonder is that any human person or persons can endure to make it. This practice of frightening with noise the evil ones of heaven (for mark you, the peoples of the Far East, unlike the Greeks, have no belief in Hades) is common to China, to Siam, to Korea, and to Burmah. The devil-jails and the devil-trees, and the professional devil-catchers, of which I have spoken before, come in importance next to the roof-beasts, and then, I think, come the prayer-poles. A prayer-pole may be a straight, symmetrical, polished piece of wood, or it may be a carelessly cut branch of a tree. In either case it is stuck in the earth a few feet from the doorway, and on it are hung prayers to the good spirits, and bits of rag, and bits of refreshment to allure and deceive the evil spirits. Sometimes a bell is hung on the top of the branch to attract the attention of both the cursers and the blessers of the land.

The good spirits that inhabit the big kingdom of Korean credulity are unfortunately lazy, and have to be rather urgently supplicated when their good services are needed. When their good services are not needed they are left, to do the Koreans justice, beautifully alone. But when the evil-doers who dwell in the Korean heaven get altogether unmanageable, the good spirits are called upon with dance and with song, with counting of rosaries and with ringing of bells, to wage war against their wicked brethren. Often the Korean angels, being Korean, go to sleep, forget to wake up, and neglect to send rain. The sending of rain is one of their few active offices. If it does not rain in Korea the rice does not grow in Korea, and then, indeed, are the Korean devils to pay. When drought falls upon Korea all Korea prays. The superstitious and the rational kneel down together, and if their united invocations fail to pierce the slumber of their well-meaning deities, then the king goes beyond the city's walls, and entering into a temple, or a sort of rustic palace that is kept in readiness for the purpose, throws himself upon the ground, and prays that his people may be blessed with rain. The rain may fall the next day, it may fall the next moon; but whenever it falls the loyal Koreans attribute it altogether to the intercession of their king. It is only when drought falls upon the land that the ordinary Korean is allowed to pray directly to most of the Korean gods. But every Korean has a household spirit—a good guardian angel of his own hearthside—to whom he may pray as often as he likes. And best beloved, most god-like, most fit to be worshipped, most fit to be prayed to, most fit to be loved of the Korean gods, and of all the Korean spirits, is one called " the blesser of little children." He is the favourite vassal of the great spirit: the phrase "great spirit" is as often upon the tongue of a Korean as upon the tongue of a North American Indian. "The blesser of little children" has under his personal charge every home in Korea. He journeys from house to house scattering blessings upon the baby heads, and forbidding evil to approach the baby people.

The Koreans emphatically believe that Korea was originally peopled by spirits and by fairies, and this belief has developed a folk-lore that is delightful and interesting in the extreme, and that often reminds us of the Norwegian folk-lore.

" When a belief rational and pure enough to be called a religion disappears, the stronger minds among the community turn in self-reliance to a belief in nothing; the weaker, in despair, to a belief in anything. This happened here; and the anything to which they turned in this case was what had never quite died out, the old aboriginal demon-worship."

And the stronger minds among the Korean community turned to the belief in nothing, which is so often called rationalism. But in Korea rationalism is tinged with, almost disguised by, that strange phenomenon of Asiatic mentality, of Asiatic belief, of Asiatic instinct called ancestor-worship.

Ancestor-worship in Korea, and ancestor-worship in China, are almost identical. The most thorough-going, the most uncompromising agnostic I ever knew was a Korean. The most thorough-going, the most uncompromising atheist I ever knew was a Chinaman, but both were staunch and uncorruptible ancestor-worshippers. Korean ancestor-worship is more than interesting, but it is merely a vassal of Chinese ancestor-worship. Like, and with Confucianism, it has come from China to Korea, and like and with Confucianism it is the mainstay of Korean morality. The worship of ancestors is an almost daily detail of Korean life. The observances of ancestor-worship are more rigidly carried out by the well-to-do Korean rationalist than by the poor superstitious Korean peasant. Death and burial mark the first, the greatest, and the most picturesque of the functions of ancestor-worship. Logically enough, the death and the interment of a child or of any unmarried person involves almost no expense, and demands no ceremonial. The infant (an unmarried man or woman of eighty is an infant in Korea) is wrapt about with the mats, the tiger skins, or the rugs upon which he died. These are wrapt about with rice straw, and the bundle is buried. That is the end of a Korean who leaves no descendants. When the father of a family dies his eldest son closes the eyes as the breath leaves the body, and the family (men and women gather together for once) let loose their hair, and shriek and sob, and, if possible, weep. So long as the dead remains in the house his relatives eat the food they like least, and as little of that as will sustain life. Indeed, the eldest son is supposed to eat nothing. Four days after the death, the members of the family redress their hair, and put on their first mourning. In Korea, as in all the Far East, mourning consists of coarse, unbleached fabrics that are commonly called, but are not quite, white. On this fourth day the family, friends, and acquaintances prostrate, prostrate, and prostrate themselves before the dead, and an exceptionally good dinner is laid beside him. Huge loaves of especially prepared bread also, and as

many kinds of fruit as the market affords—the rarer,
the more expensive, and the more hard to obtain,
the better. A dinner is also prepared for the
friends, but not for the family. About the body, and
throughout the house, candles and incense burn,
and wailing is incessant. The mourners and the
professional wailers take turns in sleeping, and
relieve each other in the audible grieving. Paper
money, that is, imitation money, and long paper
banners covered with the titles and the good
qualities of the dead, are burned. With the poor,
burial takes place five, or at the most nine days
after death. With the rich the body remains un-
buried for at least three months. Korean coffins,
like Chinese coffins, are, or are supposed to be,
air-tight. But the Korean coffin is much smaller
than the Chinese coffin, and the spaces left between the outlines of the coffin and the outlines
of the body are, in Korea, filled up with the old
clothing of the dead. If the dead had not enough
clothing, pieces of linen or of silk are added to
it. The rich Koreans usually employ a geomancer
to indicate the most auspicious day for burial.
The coffin is covered with beautiful brocaded silk,
or with beautifully carved pieces of wood.
Prayers are said almost continuously, from the
hour of death until some time after the interment.
The coffin is borne on a death-car, a unique

Korean vehicle, or by men who are hired for a small sum and who do nothing else. Beside the coffin are carried the banners, recording the rank and the virtues of the dead, and the lanterns which in life he was entitled to use. His sons follow him, in Korean mourning, and, Chinese-like, leaning heavily upon sticks. Acquaintances and friends bring up the rear, in sedan chairs and on horseback.

Korean graves are usually on hill sides, and are decorated at the utmost possible expense. Even the graves of the Korean poor are well tended, and covered with the gentle green grass, and with the soft flowers of spring, if no monument or temple is possible. But if it can be managed, a miniature temple is erected near the grave—a temple which is a shelter for those who come periodically to mourn the dead—and the grave is guarded with quaint stone images of men and other animals.

If a Korean family is unlucky they are very apt to think that one or more of their ancestors has been buried in an uncongenial spot. Then, no matter what the cost, no matter what the trouble, the grave is, or the graves are, opened, and the dead moved to some more desirable place. Korean mourning is as long or longer, as intricate or more intricate, than Chinese mourning, but so similar to Chinese mourning, which has been so often and so fully described, that it would be superfluous to here more than mention Korean mourning.

Such, then, is the religion or the irreligion of Korea. Superstition for the people; ancestor-worship for the people, the princes, and for those who are between. Strange that a nation that has driven from its midst one of the great religions of this earth, and has unrelentingly persecuted the religion of Christ, should be so devoted in its ancestor-worship. But which of us that has ever lain awake through the wordless watches of the lonely night and longed in vain—

> " For the touch of a vanished hand
>   And the sound of a voice that is still,"

shall blame the Koreans for their incessant, their blind, filial devotion ?

CHAPTER XI.

In the tenth century Korea assumed its present
boundaries, and for nine hundred years it has remained unchanged in its coast line, and its
northern limits. Except on the north, Korea is
surrounded by the sea, and its northern boundary
is marked by the Yalu and the Tiumen rivers, that
almost meet at two of their sources. For convenience in the recapitulation of Korea's history—a
recapitulation in which everything else must be
sacrificed to brevity—the history of the peninsula
may be divided into three periods : First, the
period antecedent to the final settlement of Korea's
boundaries—a period whose history is in part at
least, conjectural ; second, a period reaching from
then until modern times ; and third, a period
covering Korea's recent history, and the comparative opening up of Korea to foreign travellers, and
to foreign influence. We know as much and as
little of Korea's remotest ancestry as we do of the
ancestries of other countries. The Korean family

can trace its pedigree a long way, but at length the pedigree becomes lost in the mists of remote history and of prehistoric times, and we can form no conclusive opinion as to who were the first founders of the race.

Korean civilization came chiefly from China, and the Koreans themselves from the highlands of Manchuria and the Amoor valley.

The kingdom of Korea, and indeed the nation of Korea, was founded by an ancestor of Confucius. In Latin his name is Kicius, in Japanese it is Ki-shi, and in Chinese Ki-tsze, which means Viscount of Ki. He was a faithful vassal of the Chow dynasty of old China, and when the Chows were overthrown in 1122 B.C. he refused to acknowledge the new power, and fled with, some say five some say ten thousand followers to the north-east. Here he founded a kingdom which he called Chosön, and of which he made himself king. He was welcomed by the people already living there, and these aborigines and the followers of Ki-tsze are among the remotest ancestors to which Koreans can prove their claim. Ki-tsze introduced into his kingdom the study and the practice of medicine, agriculture, literature, the fine arts, and a dozen other industries in which China was then most proficient. He founded his kingdom on the lines of Chinese feudalism, and very much as he founded it the kingdom endured until the beginning of the Christian era, and the Koreans to-day call Ki-tsze the father of Chosön, and because of him, and the quality of his kingdom, claim that their civilization is almost as ancient as the civilization of China, and older than the civilization of Chaldea.

Just where this first kingdom of Chosön was nobody knows. Some authorities believe that it lay exactly north-west of the Yalu river, just beyond the present borders of Korea, and in the present Chinese province of Shing-king. It seems more probable that the first Chosön was in the valley of the Sungari river, and some historians, with considerable show of reason, locate it still further north, in the valley of the Amoor. Certainly its borders shrank and extended almost continually, and its entire position seems to have been more or less changed at several times, and only for a few years was any part of the Korea we know included within its area. At one time old Chosön certainly was located north-east of Pekin. It became part of China, politically and geographically, in the first century.

In the territory taken from the kings of old Chosön, and annexed to China, lay the kingdom of Kokorai. It lay east; as the old Chinese historians state, directly east, and slightly north of modern Mukden, and between the sources of the Yalu and the Sungari rivers. The people of Kokorai were warlike and able. They seem to have been rather independent of China as early as 9 A.D.; to have begun in 70 A.D. a struggle with China, which lasted until the seventh century. During this long warfare—a warfare in which their country was repeatedly invaded by the Chinese— these warlike people, instead of being conquered or exterminated by China, flourished and increased until they had overrun the peninsula of the present Korea as far as the Han river.

This, then, is the outline of the history of the western and the northern parts of modern Korea, but before turning to the history of southern and eastern Korea, it will be interesting to glance a little more particularly at the history of Kokorai.

Well, north of Kokorai, north of the Sungari river, there existed in very ancient times (if we may trust Chinese tradition) a little kingdom called To-li or Ko-rai. While one of the early kings of To-li was out hunting, a favourite waiting-maid "saw, floating in the atmosphere, a glistening vapour which entered her bosom. This ray or tiny cloud seemed to be about as big as an egg. Under its influence she conceived.

"The king, on his return, discovered her condition, and made up his mind to put her to death. Upon her explanation, however, he agreed to spare her life, but at once lodged her in prison.

"The child that was born proved to be a boy, which the king promptly cast among the pigs. But the swine breathed into his nostrils and the baby lived. He was next put among the horses, but they also nourished him with their breath, and he lived. Struck by this evident will of Heaven, that the child should live, the king listened to its mother's prayers, and permitted her to nourish and train him in the palace. He grew up to be a fair youth, full of energy, and skilful in archery. He was named ' Light of the East,' and the king appointed him master of his stables.

"One day, while out hunting, the king permitted him to give an exhibition of his skill. This he did, drawing bow with such unerring aim that the royal jealousy was kindled, and he thought of nothing but how to compass the destruction of the youth. Knowing that he would be killed if he remained in the royal service, the young archer fled the kingdom. He directed his course to the south-east, and came to the borders of a vast and impassable river, most probably the Sungari. Knowing his pursuers were not far behind him, he cried out, in a great strait,—

" ' Alas ! shall I, who am the child of the Sun,

and the grandson of the Yellow River, be stopped here powerless by this stream ? '

" So saying, he shot his arrows at the water.

" Immediately all the fishes of the river assembled together in a thick shoal, making so dense a mass that their bodies became a floating bridge. On this the young prince (and according to the Japanese version of the legend, three others with him) crossed the stream and safely reached the further side. No sooner did he set foot on land than his pursuers appeared on the opposite shore, when the bridge of fishes at once dissolved. His three companions stood ready to act as his guides. One of the three was dressed in a costume made of seaweeds, a second in hempen garments, and a third in embroidered robes. Arriving at their city, he became the king of the tribe and kingdom of Fuyu, which lay in the fertile and well-watered region between the Sungari River and the Shan Alyn, or Ever-White Mountains. It extended several hundred miles east and west of a line drawn southward through Kirin, the larger half lying on the west."

Certainly as early as 25 B.C. To-li had attained very considerable civilization. Millet, sorghum, rice, beans, and wheat grew in abundance, and were carefully cultivated. Spirits were distilled from rice and grain, as they still are in Korea,

Japan, and China. The people ate from bowls and with chop-sticks, as the people of modern China eat. The men were strong, well-built, and fearless. They were skilled in the manufacture and the use of swords, and lances, and bows and arrows. They were expert horsemen ; were fond of dancing and music ; decked themselves with pearls, and with gems of red jade. They had an elaborate system of etiquette which was rigidly observed. They had granaries, and well-built houses of wood, and their cities were surrounded by walls or palisades of stakes. They had a well-developed and a civilized religion, freer from superstition and from superstitious rites than many of the religions of modern Asia. They had a king, a well-defined feudal system, farms and farmers, nobility and serfs. They had prisons, and their system of justice was rigid. All this is surprising, for at that time the people by whom they were surrounded were barbarians, without literature, without form of government, in brief, without civilization. And yet these people of Fuyu, who were then far beyond the reach of Chinese influence, were in the full enjoyment of a civilization which was apparently of some maturity. From this many historians have inferred that the old kingdom of Fuyu was the exact site of the kingdom of Ki-tsze. This may have been. At all events, the people of Fuyu or their descendants peopled the kingdom of Kokorai, whose people in their turn populated the northern and the western parts of modern Korea.

Undoubtedly, the peoples of old Ko-rai and of Fuyu were the ancestors of the Koreans of our time. Very probably they were also the ancestors of the modern Japanese.

We know little or nothing, and we seem unlikely ever to learn much more about the early settlers of southern and eastern Korea.

Some time before the beginning of the Christian era Chinese authorities mention three independent kingdoms or nations that lay upon the shores of the Japan Sea, and south of the Han River. Early in the sixth century they had become very considerably civilized. Their literature, their art, their forms of government, and their social customs they had adopted from the Chinese. They were Buddhists; and Buddhism was then in its flower, sound in itself, and comparatively pure, and a powerful force for good and for culture. These three states were Pe-tsi (called by the Japanese historians Hiaksi), which was in the west; Sin-lo (called by the Japanese Shin-ra), which was in the south-east; and in the north, Ko-rai. They banded themselves together to attack or to repel the attacks of

China and Japan. When this was unnecessary they fought each other. They fought steadily until the tenth century. Their appetite for warfare seemed insatiable, and when they could not fight among themselves they sought foes in China and Japan, and when they could not fight the Chinese or the Japanese they picked quarrelsome wars with each other. But this period of national and international strife and of wholesale bloodshed was one of great mental and artistic activity. The civilization and the culture, and the learning of China, flowed rapidly and steadily into Korea, and through Korea into Japan.

Sin-lo, Pe-tsi, and Ko-rai appear in their origins to have had nothing in common. They were alike in being conquered by at least one alien race. Each of the three nations was greatly enriched by an influx of, and intermarriage with, Chinese, Tartars, and several other peoples of Far Asia. Their rivalry and their warfare lasted for hundreds of years; then they were united under one monarch, and slowly and surely became one nation.

The ninth and the tenth centuries were centuries of peace in Korea, and our knowledge of Korea's history during these two hundred years is most meagre. Sin-lo was then, and had been for some time, the dominant province, but the reigning

house of Sin-lo had become enervated and
incapable.   In 912 A.D. a Buddhist monk
initiated a rebellion which spread with amazing
rapidity, and was entirely successful.   The monk
proclaimed himself king, but he in his turn was
rebelled against, conquered by, and slaughtered
by a descendant of the kings of old Ko-rai, whose
name was Wang-hien, or Wang-Ken.   Wang-hien
chose Kaiseng, which was then called Sunto, as his
capital.   He became absolute monarch of the whole
peninsula, and gave back to it its ancient name of
Ko-rai.   Kai-seng is but a short distance north-
east of Söul, and so the first capital of united, and
possibly the last capital of united Korea, are
but a stone's throw from each other.   A war
which shortly occurred with the Kitan Tartars,
who lived west of the Yalu River, resulted in a
change of frontier, the Kitans taking and holding
most of the north-western territory of Korea.
From that day to this the boundaries of Korea
have practically remained unchanged, and this
brings us to the second period of Korea's history.

Four hundred years of peace now fell upon
Korea.   These four were the most brilliant
centuries in Korea's history.   Feudalism gave
place to absolute monarchy, and the peninsula
was divided into eight provinces, over each of
which the king placed a governor.   Buddhism

became the national religion ; temples, pagodas, monasteries, nunneries in the best forms of Chinese architecture, and in Chinese-like, but better than Chinese forms of architecture, were built everywhere.   The naturally rich resources of the peninsula were developed, augmented, and made the most of, and a flourishing trade was driven with both of the rival kingdoms—China and Japan.   But China still remained the fountain-head of Korean learning and culture. The wealthy and the noble Koreans sent their sons to China to be educated.   This was the period of the Sung dynasty in China—the wonderful period of Chinese literature and art to which I referred a chapter or two ago.   Korea, which was then more abjectly the vassal of China in culture, in letters, in art, and in sociology, than she was politically, followed as fast as she could in the footsteps of China's literary and artistic progress. It was then that Korea first became deeply interested in Chinese classics, and from then until now a thorough knowledge of the Chinese classics has been, and is, the supreme test of Korean education and culture.   Then the Koreans first learned to print, printing from raised letters cut in blocks of wood.   Toward the close of these memorable four hundred years it is said that there were more books, more printed books in Korea than there were inhabitants. It was then that general education became a matter of course in the peninsula. It was then, as I have said, that Korean art was at its best and broadest; and it was then that the Korean alphabet was invented, or at least became generally used. Many scholars maintain even now that the Korean is the most beautiful, and the most sensible alphabetical system that the world has, or ever has had.

Early in the fourteenth century the Mongols had begun their run of unprecedented conquest. Khublai Khan and Genghis Khan, the mightiest Mongols of their time, determined to conquer the earth. Their ideas of the extent of the earth were limited, very limited, but within the narrow limits of those ideas they very approximately carried out their bold intentions. Korea was completely subdued.

The history of Korea during the period of the Mongolian supremacy in China is a history of entire subjection. Toward the decadence of the power of the Mongols Korea was called upon to conquer Japan, but escaped from the farce of trying to do so. For the Mongol was already tottering on his throne. The Mongols most in power were quarrelling among themselves, and plotting against each other, and the people whom they ruled had grown dissatisfied enough (as the

Chinese once in a very great while do), to not only contemplate but execute a rebellion. During the last days of the Mongol's already shattered power Korea was almost free from Chinese supervision, and altogether free from Chinese control; for China had more than she could do at home. At last a Chinese monk, a Buddhist priest, calling himself Ming, or "Bright," pushed the insecurely seated Mongol from his throne. This priest proclaimed himself, and the people acclaimed him, the Emperor and Deliverer of China. He married that he might found a dynasty. The first Ming was indeed a man of might, and the period during which he and his descendants were supreme in China is peculiarly interesting to the student of Korean history. For it was during this period that the Koreans copied the Chinese Mings; assumed the dress in all its details which they have worn ever since, and many of their most characteristic customs. When the Mongols fell, the king of Korea, who seems to have been an exceptionally good sort, wished to give his onetime masters sanctuary in his hermit kingdom, but a greater than the king—a powerful courtier named Ni Taijō—disallowed the king's judgment, dethroned the king, imprisoned him, and usurped, or at least ascended, the Korean throne, and established the present Korean dynasty. That was five hundred, or to be exact, five hundred and three years ago. The name of the peninsula was again changed, and it was re-named Ta Chō-sun. Söul, which he called, and which in fact we ought to call, Han-yang, was made the capital. And it was then that the famous wall of Söul was built, and then that her imposingly wide streets were laid out and made. Ni Taijō changed the boundaries of Korea's eight provinces. Those boundaries have not been changed since. It was during his reign that the pale blue, which we carelessly and generally call white, became the colour of every ordinary Korean dress. It was then that the Korean hat in all its glory was born. It was then that the Korean top-knot was erected upon Korean heads. It was then that Buddhism made way for Confucianism ; and it was then that the gaining of office or position of trust was deter-mined solely by the result of competitive literary examinations. And it was then that the Koreans invented, as they did invent, in their part of the world at least, the art of printing by movable and cast metal type.

Again Korea had peace, peace for two hundred years. Then like the Romans of old the Koreans who, like them, had feasted and lounged too much, became enervated and thriftless. Japan grew bolder, and for more than a quarter of a century

Korea was constantly ravaged by pirates and piratical armies from the islands of Japan. In 1592 Konishi and Kato devastated large tracts of Korea, and it was after their final expulsion, after the final expulsion of the power of which they were powerful units, that (as I mentioned before) according to many historians, religion fell in Korea into the disgrace from which it has never arisen. Ping-yang was the site of many of the most desperate struggles that took place between the natives and the invaders. All through Chosön's history Ping-yang has been the battle-field of a large proportion of the most desperate conflicts that have taken place on Korean soil. In 1597 the Japanese made their second invasion of Korea. It was during this invasion that the Japanese seized upon vast quantities of Korean treasure and of art works—works of art which, transplanted to the fertile soil of Japan, quickly took root, and became the seed-plants of a con- siderable portion of Japan's best art.

During this second Japanese invasion China, in answer to Korean prayers, sent vast reinforcements to the aid of the Chosönese. For seven years Korea suffered from fire, from pillage, from war, from pestilence, and from famine, and her already depleted resources were drained with the necessity of feeding and sheltering, wily-nily, two great alien armies. A million Koreans died during these seven years; a million, beyond the normal death-rate, of men were killed in battle, or died after battle, or succumbed to starvation, or one of the dire diseases bred of war, and in war-time. The sun of Korea's greatness set then, and never since have the Koreans been able to say, or to approximately say,—

'Now is the sun upon the high-most hill of our national day's journey.'

Korea struggled, struggled bravely enough, to retrieve her fallen fortunes, but before her old wounds were healed new ones were inflicted. Beyond the mountains that marked, and still mark, her northern boundaries a mighty race had risen—a race that became supreme in China as in Korea, and a race that only now seems in danger of extermination or degradation. The Manchius dwelt where the people of old Fuyu had dwelt. They conquered Korea, and then they conquered China. In 1627 the Manchius practically mastered Chosön; and ten years later they so completely humbled the King of Korea that he acknowledged as his master the Manchiu Emperor, who was now supreme in Pekin, and the Korean King covenanted to send four times a year to the Tartar an enromous tribute, and the Koreans bound themselves to perform to the Tartar and to his representatives the kow-tow which has played so ridiculous a part in our European difficulties with China, and to sing hymns of praise commemorative of the Manchius' generosity and graciousness in not having wiped Korea from off the face of the Asiatic earth. Let me quote a short paragraph from an historian who never appears over-partial to China :—

" Aside from the entrance at stated times of the imperial envoy to collect the tribute, and the annual embassy of Korean nobles to Pekin to do homage to ' the Great Khan,' the internal politics of ' the little outpost state ' were not interfered with by the Chinese Government."

Should Japan become the mistress of Korea; should Japan become the mistress of China—will she, I wonder, be as magnanimous ?

Twenty years brought little or no change to the people of Chosön. In 1653 Hamel was wrecked upon the Korean shores, and what I have quoted from his memoirs indicates, by no means sufficiently, but as sufficiently as my space will allow me to indicate, the condition of Korea from then until 1777. And in 1777 begins the history of modern Korea.

That history affords neither pleasant writing nor pleasant reading to any one of European or Europeanly-American birth. Korea is hardly enough placed with China on the one hand and Japan on the other, but for all that she, perhaps because she has been the weakest and the most exposed of Oriental countries, has suffered most from—no, I do not mean suffered, but been most at the mercy of Europe. "Courtesy with the East, respect to the West, tribute to them both, and no foreigners wanted in the kingdom," was Korea's political creed when Korea ceased to be one of the intrinsically great nations of the past, and become one of the unjustly unimportant nations. During the last hundred or hundred and twenty years Korea has changed but little centrifugally, but centripetally she has changed, well—considering that she is Asiatic—enormously. Christianity, in an insidious Portuguese sort of way, had peeped into Korea many years before, but now Christianity is forcibly injected into Korea, injected in a way of which, however admirable it may seem to us, Christ would never have approved. Christianity, the species of Christianity offered to Korea, has not flourished there, and the nice, new Occidental civilization which was offered to Korea a year after the patriarchs of Massachusetts perfumed the Bay of Boston with tea-leaves, seems to have been rather a failure in the Land of the Morning Calm.

About the Jesuit fathers who sneaked into

Korea under the shelter of the big hats that Korean widowers wear, and about the American and English missionaries who laid down their lives, and who have amplified and luxuriated their lives in Korea, I should like to say a good deal, but when one cannot say all that one might say and wishes to say, it is perhaps least stupid to say nothing.   But to those who would like to study Christian missions in the East I would first of all recommend Mr. Curzon's " Problems of the Far East," and then, as far as Korea is concerned, I would recommend the works of the missionaries Griffis and Ross.

Korea itself has undergone little change since Hamel escaped from Korea.   Korea has suffered during those years a good deal of change at the hands of others, a change that is, I think, not altogether to our credit.   An American commodore opened Japan up to the West, and now (so at least they tell me), Japan is threatening to annihilate the West.   Another American commodore, rather a noisier man, and not blessed with so fortunate a field of action, opened modern Korea to nineteenth century Europe and nineteenth century North America.   Since then, the history of Korea has been a history of Korean degeneration, and European and United States advancement.   The King of Korea has become a patron of telephones, and the hero of innumerable magazine articles—magazines published on both sides of the Atlantic.

Such is the outline of Korea's history—hurried, dry, and incomplete; so incomplete, indeed, that it is not in truth an outline but rather scraps of outline. But Korea's history is anything but dry, if we study it in something like intelligible entirety.

One who reads only English—or even the languages of modern Europe—but wishes to know Korean history in some detail, will be forced to do considerable literary browsing. A full and altogether satisfactory history of Korea has yet to be written in English. Its writing would involve years of earnest work, and could only be accomplished by one thoroughly familiar with the Chinese language and Chinese literature. In the meantime there is much interesting information to be found in periodicals, in English papers printed in Shanghai, and to be gleaned from Blue-books.

Both Ross and Griffis have contributed valuably to our literature *re* Korea. But neither of them are the easiest of reading, and both write from a sectarian, if not a narrow point of view. No one who is interested in Korea can afford not to read Curzon's " Problems of the Far East," Lowell's " Chosön," Carles' " Life in Korea," and almost above all Dallet's "*Histoire de l'Église de Corée.*"   And don't forget dear, quaint old Hamel. There are more to be by-all-means read, but not many, and in reading one we shall learn the titles of others.

The chapter headed "Korea," in "The Life of Sir Harry Parkes" is, like all the other chapters in that admirable work, delightfully written, and peculiarly interesting. Korea has been rather cruelly used—it seems to me—but it is pleasant to feel that in connection with Korea, England has little or no cause to reproach herself.

CHAPTER XII.

THE SCOURGES OF CHINA.

IT is the present war between China and Japan that has brought Korea to our general notice; has caused us to ask and learn something of where and what Korea is. It is this war that will largely open up Korea, directly or indirectly, to Occidental travellers, to Occidental adventurers, and to Occidental enterprise.

Whatever the ultimate effect of the war upon Japan the effect will be far greater upon Korea, greater even than it will be upon China. China is a huge place, and will, I think, change but slowly, no matter how great her defeat may be, no matter how many and how sweeping the concessions she may perforce yield to Japan. Korea is small and weak, and may, if force enough is brought to bear upon her, change swiftly.

Korea has been now almost lost sight of in the present struggle; because it has ceased to be the theatre of the strife. But the war concerns Korea no whit less than it concerns China and Japan.

This war is an essential part of Korea's history—the most recent scene in Korea's dramatic life.

With the war in the details of its action we are all very familiar, at this moment. But I doubt if we are quite *au courant* of the causes of the war; and we have yet much to learn of the two interesting peoples who are waging the war.

There are several reasons why China fell a fighting of Japan—China had to, for Japan forced the war—China hates Japan—China, an important part of China, was unnerved by a fearful plague and easily excited into indulging in the dissipation of war. It was easy and comparatively safe for Japan to make China fight, because China had for years so neglected the art of war (if so holy a name may be attached to so often so unholy a thing), that she was ill prepared to cope with any foe that was more than a foe of straw; was ill prepared but did not know it. The Chinese for long have not regarded warfare as the manliest of occupations. Scholars, not soldiers, are their beau ideals, and the scum of their populace fills the ranks of their standing army. Their officers know little of military tactics, and are wont to direct, from behind the curtains of palanquins, the actions of their troops.

Japan has fallen a fighting of China because she hates China; because she dearly loves a bit of glory, and saw a splendid chance to gain it; and because she too felt the need of a national stimulant : the course of her true politics had not been flowing over smoothly, and she had been badly unnerved by earthquake.

China is the home of the wild white roses, of supreme philosophy, and of deadly pestilence. The recent plague in Hong Kong and Canton was merely an outbreak of an inevitably recurrent pest which is the sure result of the conditions of Chinese life. We are railing loudly just now against Chinese dirt. I feel that Chinese dirt is very much less than Chinese poverty. And it is a significant fact that the dirt and the poverty are usually found together. The houses and grounds of the rich Chinese that I have known in Singapore, in Penang, in Shanghai, and in Hong Kong, have been models of order and neatness, if not (according to European standards) of beauty.

The poorer quarters of the Chinese cities are undeniably filthy. But it is the filth bred of over-crowding and of dire penury, and of the inability of the government to cope with such enormous masses of humanity, rather than of natural uncleanliness. It is an almost infallible rule that only lazy people are dirty ; sloth and filth are old bedfellows. The Chinese are the most industrious, thrifty nation on our globe ; and I am convinced that the national dirt, the dirt of the poorer classes, is their misfortune and not their fault.

But there the dirt is, and, like a thousand maggot-breeding filth-heaps, it is constantly creating horrid germs of deadly disease.

It is very much to our national shame that the Chinese quarters of Hong Kong are almost as filthy as the poorer parts of Canton. We are absolute in Hong Kong; but we have done disgracefully little for the sanitation of the native quarters in the island we have conquered.

And yet Hong Kong ought to be the healthiest city in the world, the freest from pestilence. I know of no other city so admirably situated for conditions of health. Aside from the beauty of the place, and regarding it only as adaptable to healthy modes of human life and residence, it is ideal. And our flag waves over Hong Kong. And yet but yesterday a plague was raging there; only to think of which must make the gorge of Christendom rise.

While the plague raged, no doubt everything was done that terror and wisdom could devise. But the evil is deep-rooted, and it will not be uprooted in an hour.

Except for their unavoidable proximity to the possibility of dire disease (in which the Chinese are born, live, and die), the European inhabitants of Hong Kong are in every way to be envied.

Alas! almost the latest duty of the *doyen* of that Queen's house was the sending of a disinfecting party through the plague-stricken districts of Hong Kong—a party including British soldiers, some of whom were attacked by the seemingly invincible plague, and died a death almost Chinese in its horror.

The conditions of well-to-do Chinese life are very pleasant in Hong Kong.

But in the Hong Kong of the poor there is nothing much but a tragic struggle for human existence, and misery, misery almost unalleviated, and yet not quite unalleviated. The poorest, hardest pressed of the Chinese have—more than most peoples—the love of home, the joy in work, the affection for kith and kin that go far to alleviate any lot, however hard. And they have other blessings—the poverty-cursed Chinese—they have their festivals and their temples. The cobbler, who sits by the wayside and works for a few sen, smokes now and again his tiny pipe of opium ; he burns his incense sticks and his red, paper prayers in the joss-house, and once in every four years he contributes some mite of work, of treasure, or of interest to the Soul festival.

Plagues fall upon China almost with a grim regularity; they crush into terrible graves countless thousands. But China goes on, and the Chinese go on; and, ignorant as they may often be of the laws of sanitation, they remain for ever steadfast to themselves and to their country, and to what they conceive to be for the best advantage of both. What nation does more?

We have made many conquests in the East. But we have not been altogether victorious over Asiatic disease. We have carried our flag in triumph into the Chinaman's Mecca—into Pekin. And we have knocked open the doors of the emperor's palace, knocked them open with the butts of our rifles. We have made Shamien our own. We have made it bloom like a fair English garden, and at the very gate of Canton; where it lies a mute but eloquent reproach to the filth of the Chinese city. We have gained the probably most beautifully situated city in the world—the city of Hong Kong—and there we have built for our soldiers an almost ideal barrack. But we have been powerless—we are powerless to-day against the relentless outbreak of a Chinese plague. And Shamien—that proud spot of our, perhaps, supremest Chinese triumph—reeks with the poisonous stench that comes from Canton.

Alas! alas! We have paid a high price for

our occupancy of Asia. We have often sacrificed
to her our children.

The history of China is spotted with plagues.
And the sanitary condition of many of the
Chinese cities and the density of their populations
are such that we can scarcely hope for China a
future much freer from such plagues than her past
has been.

Go into the native market in Hong Kong; see
the burning sun pour down upon the half putrid
fish and a hundred unwholesome looking native
foods; see the dense, sweating, seething human
mass that is packed in among the stalls, and you
will wonder that Hong Kong is ever free from
pestilence. But the European residents of Hong
Kong are not, as a rule, over familiar with the
details of the native quarter. They live on the
Peak, or on the outskirts of the beautiful public
gardens, where no smells reach them coarser than
the indescribable perfume of the wisteria.

Nothing could be lovelier, happier than Hong
Kong the European. It is a place of charming
bungalows, of superb verdure, a place of green
hills and of fanning breezes, a place of shady
streets and sweetly fragrant nooks.

Nothing could be more picturesque, nothing
could be sadder than most of Hong Kong the
Chinese. It is a crowded place of deepest

poverty. When I have said that, I have said it all.

As I have said, the Chinese are not, I believe, greatly responsible for either the gravity or the frequency of their epidemics. Poverty, extreme poverty, commits most of the crimes against the Chinese health. People who are too poor to buy soap cannot wash themselves, and much less their clothes. People who can afford none of the necessities of health cannot be blamed for falling ill. And the Chinese government, which is at the fountain head the most paternal of all governments (but corrupt in many of its branches), is unable to cope with the unavoidable poverty of China's overplus of humanity in those parts of the empire in which the population is densest and most congested. It is a common mistake to suppose that there are more people in China than China could support if those people were equally scattered over her vast territory. But in the great centres of Chinese life the people are overcrowded to starvation and to pestilence.

Yes; things seem to be going rather badly in Asia just now—Mahommedan and Hindoo strife, mysterious and ominous mango smearing, native regimental insubordination, and buried treasure that refuses to be dug up, are rife in India and Burmah. Siam is slowly, but I fear surely, disappearing within the insatiable maw of France. China has been smitten down by a dire plague. Japan has been torn with earthquake: and now a black war cloud has broken over the Far East, drenching with its deadly rain of bullets Korea, China, and Japan.

For centuries Korea has given China and Japan an excuse to exchange discourtesies, and to vent a spleen, which for many hundreds of years has sometimes slept, but never slept soundly, and much less died.

The Koreans have never of recent years been skilful in averting calamity from themselves or from their country. The Japanese are as brave as they are venturesome. The knight errant spirit that characterized old feudal Japan has by no means died out of Japan the new, probably never will die out of Japan. It is "bone of her bone, flesh of her flesh." The land which was for so many decades the theatre of that dignified but horrible butchery called Hari-Kari, is not the land of cowards. Hari-Kari, or self-disembowelment, was looked upon in old Japan as a ceremonial of more than religious importance. And, even now, numbers of the Japanese deplore the abolition of Hari-Kari. It follows that the Japanese are neither afraid to die, nor reluctant to fight against fearful odds. But it is China who is fighting against fearful odds now. And yet I venture to think that in the long run Japan will lose more, gain less than her adversary. The Chinese are slow to anger. They are slower to forgive. They are not fond of withdrawing from any position they have taken. They are not prone to look at things through the eyes of others. They are not easy to convince. The Chinese in things military are shockingly behind the times, and the Japanese are splendidly up-to-date. But there are qualities that are, in the long run, more apt to win an Oriental war than being up-to-date.

China may cry, "Peccavi," but she won't mean it. Unless, indeed, she be permanently crippled she will bide her time, watch her opportunity, and fight again and to better purpose. Japan is China's natural foe. China has forgiven us, I verily believe, for forcing ourselves into Pekin and for wresting from her Hong Kong. But she will never forgive Japan. And why should she? Shame to any nation that forgives a Port Arthur!

In half a day the Japanese can steam from their own coast to Korea: but also any Power in possession of Korea can steam from there to Japan as quickly. Korea is certainly more necessary to Japan than to China. But geographical propinquity does not necessarily constitute territorial right; and so far as we can judge the merits and demerits of so perplexed, so involved, so almost prehistoric, so Oriental a question, China has more right to Korea than Japan has. But international right is fast becoming (if it has not already become) a matter of national might, and concerning Korea the question of the moment is not, as it was a few months ago, "Who will fight the better, China or Japan?" but "How far shall we let them fight?"

Russia has her eye upon Korea. Even the United States may crave to stick a finger, a modest little finger, in this political pie.

What right have we to interfere in the quarrels of Eastern Powers? What right have we? It is too late for us to think of that now. We have kinsfolk in all those Oriental places, and shall have in the generations to come. It is our supreme duty to protect them, even though to do that 'great right we do a little wrong.' Russia securely, strongly lodged in Korea would not be an altogether desirable sight for British eyes.

And Korea, where does she come in in the present quarrel? Alas, she bids fair to go out, unless indeed Europe should be sentimentally chivalrous and forbid the disnationalization of one of the few remaining unchanged countries of the old Eastern world, and decree that Korea should remain yet a little longer a steadfast landmark upon the ever shifting sands of history.

What rights have the Koreans in the matter? Alas, it is also too late to ask that question. Their rights seem very apt to be torn into shreds between the dragons of China and Japan, or else to be (as most Eastern rights are) crushed into dust beneath the heavy but righteous foot of advancing civilization.

CHAPTER XIII.

JAPAN is ungrateful. She always has been, and, I fear, always will be. She has achieved over an adversary, in most essentials abler than herself, a brilliant run of, at least temporary, victories, largely because she has adopted Western methods of warfare; and now she is celebrating the victory of her European-borrowed arms by slapping Europe in the face. How very like a woman! How very like Japan!

The Emperor of Japan has politely informed us—cautiously informed us through the Japanese minister in Washington—that we must please mind our own business, for "no offer of mediation on the part of a third Power would be accepted by Japan until her object, which was to crush the power of China, had been completely attained."

And it is being more or less openly said (I believe the authority I quote to be entirely reliable) on the streets of Yokohama: "When we've finished China we must teach one of the big European Powers a lesson. England, for instance, thinks a great deal too much of herself and not half enough of us." If Japan is really ambitious for a war with England, let us hope that she will soon find an excuse for it. The sooner such warfare is waged the better—for China—and it will not greatly inconvenience us.

Japan has drunk of the awful, red wine of war, and the wine has gone to her pretty little head. Let us hope that she will not have too much of a headache in the inevitable morning, and that she may, for the near future at least, have the good sense to drink our health and her own in the beverages that best suit her: a cup of tea and a wee thimbleful of saki.

There are two reasons why Japan has so far triumphed over China, reasons which prove Japan our debtor ; and yet Japan has, as far as we are concerned, borne her honours so badly that it deserves at least our passing attention.

Compare China and Japan on the map ; compare their populations and it certainly seems that by this time the Chinese Goliath should have crushed and appropriated the Japanese David. But maps don't tell us everything, and figures lie, if we ask them to say more than they ought.

Figures are excellent things, if we permit them to mind their own business. But they are not philosophers ; they are not logicians. Then, too, David always has so many advantages over Goliath. David can get about so much quicker. He can move his body sooner than the giant can move one limb. His hand can receive the message sent it by his brain in a fraction of the time that the same transaction takes Goliath.

Perhaps we have all—those of us who are surprised at China's at least momentary defeat—been looking too much upon the surface, taking a too topographical view of the situation. Bulk is not always a blessing. It may become an embarrassment. It is, at any rate, often misleading. The size of China, and its vast population have been misleading to many of us who have had more interest in the present Chino-Japanese war than knowledge of China and Japan.

I call the war the Chino-Japanese war, because it is a Chino-Japanese war. Korea is the excuse for the war, not the cause of the war. Poor, picturesque, badly-used place, let us pray that she may not be too the victim, altogether the, victim of the war.

China has been, so far at least, quite unable to mobilize her forces. Japan—who is the art concentration of many nations—has concentrated her comparatively small, but altogether fine forces, concentrated them with a nicety and a shrewdness that might well be a lesson to the Europe from which she has learned her art of war.

The Art of War! Japan seems indeed to be making War a fine art—but, alas! she is making it, no less than it has always been, a butchery!

There is, however, an underlying fact, which seems to me to account above everything else— yes, and to account philosophically—for the humbling of China, and the swift advance of Japan. The Chinese are creative as a race; the Japanese are imitative. A creative nature is self-reliant; and an imitative nature is, of necessity, self-doubtful. China has been inclined to rely upon herself; Japan has doubted herself and relied upon Europe. China's strength has been China's weakness; the weakness of Japan has proven Japan's strength. It is true that China has bought ships and guns from Europe; that she has borrowed officers to drill her soldiers, and to manage her ships; but all this has been done in a spirit of disallowance. She has always believed in herself. To her, all the rest of the world is, as it was to ancient Rome, "barbarian."

Japan lacking, as a nation, the creative faculty,

possesses, more eminently than any other nation, the imitative faculty. Her art is borrowed from China and Korea; her methods of government, and her methods of war from that Western world to which she has so lately, for the first time, opened her gates. Japan is victorious to-day because of her self-distrust, and because of her eager and compliant imitation of Western methods. China is defeated to-day because of her half-hearted adoption of European ways and means.

Japan jumps at conclusions with the swift intelligence of a bright woman. China proves, and proves again, the worth of any custom or method that she adopts. Japan improves everything that she adopts. China is more like a wise man, she understands everything that she adopts. China is the slower, but China is the surer.

Japan has so far had the best of the fight, because she has imitated us, and because she has been able to mobilize her forces.

Whether the present war will suddenly break through the thick crust of Chinese self-sufficiency, of Chinese bigotry, of Chinese hatred of change, remains to be seen. If it does, China may swiftly regain her lost ground. In any event it is not probable that so thoughtful, so wise, so reasonable a people as the Chinese will fail to sooner or later learn thoroughly the lesson which this present war preaches to them. Perhaps in a few months, perhaps in twenty or thirty years, but surely sometime, China will learn how right Galileo was, how decidedly the world does move, and how needful it is that we who live on the world, should move with the world. Then we may all learn how great a people the Chinese really are; how vastly superior in many ways to their more fascinating, more artistic, but less stable neighbours—the Japanese.

I am not, I know, taking a popular view of the relative admirableness of China and Japan; but I believe that I take the true view. It is a view diametrically opposed to the concensus of European opinion, but it is not a view altogether original with me. A number of eminent men, who have spent some of the best years of their lives in China and Japan, compare the two peoples quite as much to the advantage of China as I have ventured to do. In 1882 Herr von Brandt, who was then the German minister to Pekin, who had previously been in office in Tokio, an able diplomat, and a man greatly valued by Sir Harry Parkes, wrote to Sir Harry:—" The news you gave me about the treaty revision has interested me much. For my part I would see no objection to the institution of a kind of mixed court for all cases in which Japanese were concerned, provided the judges were elected from a certain number of persons nominated by the Treaty Powers. The proposal to submit foreigners to the Japanese police jurisdiction seems inadmissible; conflicts of all kinds and gravity would, in my opinion, be the immediate consequences of such a concession. In general it seems to me that the Japanese have done nothing which could entitle them to the concessions they demand, and that the experience of the past hardly authorizes any far-going experiment for the future; the fact that Japanese jurisdiction is at the present moment as bad as bad can be can hardly be given as a reason to extend it over those who are not subjected to it for the present. The opening of the country to foreign trade can hardly be considered as a fair equivalent, as the Japanese, if the measure is carried out, are certain to reap much more benefit from it than the foreigners will ever do. After all, I am glad that it is not my business to put the Japanese world right again : with all their faults there is much more steadiness and logic in the Chinese than in their high flightinesses the sons of the land of the Rising Sun."

Yes; the Japanese have a graceful knack of quietly getting the best of most bargains, and certainly the opening of the Japanese treaty ports to Europeans has, as regards everything but art, benefited Japan far more than it has benefited Europe. Herr von Brandt's prophecy has been more than fulfilled, and that gives some little weight to his opinion that there is more steadiness and logic in the Chinese than in the Japanese.

Sir Harry Parkes had as much cause as man well could have to hate the Chinese; and yet, again and again, he has felt impelled to utter some testimony in their favour. On the fourteenth of December, 1874, he wrote to Sir D. Brooke Robertson :—" I think our views resemble very closely on the China-Japan question, now of the past fortunately. The luck has fallen to Japan, who certainly did not deserve it. I can't help feeling sorry to see the old country opposite give in, when she had right on her side, to this youngster among nations."

How history repeats itself! Twenty years ago the war cloud that hung over China and Japan was fanned away by the temperate winds of European advice, absorbed in the sunshine of common sense. To-day the storm of war has burst over Further Asia, burst in splendid, awful fury; and the Chinese and Japanese are slaying each other by the shoal. We have taught them how to do it. And the Chinese Goliath lies smitten (smitten almost to death, at least so his enemy seems to think), by the well directed pebbles of Japan. Of the effect of the successive and reportedly crushing blows administered by Japan to her colossal neighbour, it is, of course, too early to speak with confidence. Success means so much to China, that should the present run of ill luck continue, the downfall of the reigning dynasty would not be surprising. A victorious Japanese army in the streets of Pekin would almost inevitably so result. Let us hope that China—China the picturesque, China the beautiful—will not be bowed so low as that. Our own interests in the Orient would suffer materially through such a radical disturbance of the balance of power. For our own sake, and for the sake of right, it is to be hoped that China will be spared the humiliation of opening the gates of her sacred and capital city to an invading army from Japan. That would be the saddest misfortune that has ever befallen China : sadder far than the misfortune that befell her when we took from her the island of Hong Kong, and flew our flag above the dragon on the imperial palace at Pekin. But so long as Japan is essentially stronger in army and in navy than China, China must submit, with what grace she can, to defeat. But having learned from us how to fight, it really is too bad of Japan to turn up at us her pretty, little, yellow nose, to shake her flower-crowned head at us in derision, or to make it uncomfortable for our countrymen and women within her gates.

This is as true of the Japanese to-day as when Sir Harry Parkes wrote it twenty years ago :— "The Japanese have committed the error of believing all that they have been told about themselves and increasing this by their own imagination, and the result is that their own little island is too small to hold them."

At this moment Japan evidently believes that her present victories are attributable more to her own skill and prowess than to her exact and servile adoption of European methods and models, and so she is tossing her head and treating us a little rudely.

Ah, well! we all have to learn some sharp lessons, whether we are individuals or nations. China is learning such a lesson now. I wonder whose turn it will be next—Japan's ?

This, at least, when next Japan fights let us hope that she may have become Europeanized enough not to wage war before she declares it.

Ingratitude seems to me to have been the trait most pronounceably shown by the Japanese during this present struggle. And the desire of some Japanese women to join the army as combatants seems to me the most amusing incident in a war

that has had more than one funny side to it.   But
there is one other thing to have been noticed about
Japan of late : a thing that seems to have rather
escaped notice—Japan is trembling.

In the glowing moment of her supreme victories,
in this long hour of her almost unprecedented run
of luck, does it seem more stupid, or more imper-
tinent to speak of Japan as being a-tremble ?   The
laws of some countries hold that truth is no libel.
The laws of other countries hold that truth is the
greatest libel.   I am uttering libel or I am not
uttering libel, according to the country by whose
laws I may be judged.   Most emphatically, I am
uttering the truth.   No other word so truly
adjectives Japan as does the word trembling.

This is the age of earthquakes.   Almost daily
the papers record the upheaval of some part or
other of the world.   And earthquakes are becoming almost common where they used to be nearly
or quite unheard of.   Japan, as far we know, always
has been, and probably always will be, the strong-
hold of earthquakes.   That inscrutable some one
whom some of us call God ; that inscrutable something which some of us call Fate ; that inscrutable
some one or something of which the bravest of us,
the most phlegmatic of us, the most callous of us, one
and all, stand in more than wholesome dread ; for
uncountable centuries, has seen fit, and will see fit,

to hold over the flower-crowned head of Japan a Damoclean sword. The thread by which that sword is held is very much frailer than the thread that, in the classic days of old Greece, held that sword's prototype. It breaks, does the Japanese thread. It breaks very often. It breaks with a persistent irregularity that is almost regular in its frequency. And Japan is disembowelled with a Hari-Kari far more terrible, far more merciless than the Hari-Kari which used to be the glory of the well-born criminals, or the well-born unfortunates of old Japan.

The first time I ever saw a Japanese earthquake (and I have had the misfortune to see many), it occurred to me that the Japanese, who create nothing, who imitate and ornament everything, had caught from the brutal butchery of Nature (Nature who is worshipped in Japan, as she is worshipped almost nowhere else), the idea of that terrible self-annihilation which was for centuries the gruesome glory of Japan. Japan is the pet lamb of Nature, the favourite home of art, the chosen throne of beauty, and yet the Japanese always have had the greatest enthusiasm for the horrible in Nature, and the horrible in art.

Nature is, perhaps, the most convenient term by which we, who believe in God, we who believe in Fate, and we who believe in nothing, can agree to

commonly express our common wish to personify
that of which none of us know too much, but of
which we all think, more or less, and of which
most of us wish to speak rather frequently.

I have called Japan the pet child of Nature, and
so she is. Not all the earthquakes that have ever
out-canniballed the cannibals; not all the earthquakes that ever swallowed houses and gulped
down humans, could counterbalance the enormous
partiality which Nature shows for Japan. Never
bloomed such flowers, never grew such trees, never
did such moonlight, with such dappled gold and
silver, glorify such landscapes. Verily doth Nature
love Japan as she loves no other spot on earth.
Out of the great womb of Nature Japan was born,
and truly every star in heaven danced and shone
the brighter. But Nature, like many another
mother, seems to have overtaxed herself in giving
to the world so sublime a child. The umbilical
cord has never been cut between Nature and
Japan. The Japanese have never ceased to suck
the wonderful milk of Nature, the milk that has
nourished in them their great love for the beautiful,
their great appreciation of the beautiful, and their
supreme gift of reproducing the beautiful. But all
this seems to have worn on Nature. The mother
who nurses her child beyond a physically reasonable period invariably suffers. The child may

thrive, but the mother grows ill : most women who are ill are hysterical. Nature, if there is such a thing as Nature, is a mother. Nature, if there is such a thing as Nature, is a woman. Nature is a mother, because from Nature have we, all parts of our world, and all other worlds, been born. Nature is a woman, because no manly thing could be so cruel to its offspring as Nature is. The child is so over-grown, so hungry, so perpetually demanding of, draining Nature, that Nature, veriest woman that she is, must needs, once in a way, lose patience with Japan.

But save for her momentary losses of temper, Nature is to Japan the tenderest of mothers, fashioning for her, as all mothers love to fashion for their favourite children, the daintiest of gar- ments. And never yet did pet child wear such fine frocks, such robes of soft but splendid beauty, as Nature makes, year in year out, season in season out, for Japan. She weaves them of flowers, she buckles them with brilliant berries, and she sprays them with a drench of soft, warm, unsoiling, and altogether incomparable perfume. She sings sweet songs of mother-love to her pet child. Such lul- labies she croons to it ! She keeps for it the most wonderful of orchestras. An orchestra that makes ceaseless, but everchanging music. Hum- ming birds wing notes of music into that marvellous concerto, silver rills "that gush out i' the midst of roses," waterfalls that in the moonlight and in the sunlight kiss the moss-warmed rocks, and leap in passionate ecstasy into the arms of the flower-dressed earth, drip liquid notes of beauty into that wondrous symphony. The wings of butterflies add falsetto, but, oh! so sweet, notes, and the wind, as it wantons between the wanton trees, and kisses the fragrant flowers, steals from them their honey, and adds perfume unto perfume, and music unto music, until Japan, Nature's pet baby, cuddles down into the warm eider-down of its cradle, an eider-down that is incomparably soft with flower-petals, and that smells of blossoms that are sweeter than music.

Nature does ten hundred gracious, gentle, mother-kindnesses to Japan, and Japan accepts them all, and asks for more, and then Nature, well, Nature's nerves give out, and as many another mother, who has an almost idolatrous love for her child, has done, Nature gives Japan a fearful shaking. When Nature recovers herself a bit, and sees what she has done, she is always very sorry, and about the tumbled, broken, paper houses, through the ruined fields of paddy and of rice, over the heaps of torn and burned wisteria, well, she does what mothers have done before her, she stoops and kisses the place that she has made sting, she scatters violets over her pet child's bruises, she makes vines, blue with blossom and purple with perfume, grow over the marks which she has made upon the dimpled limbs and the pretty features of her favourite, but somewhat trying child.

But a kiss never yet altogether made up for a blow. Our children forgive us our cruelties, but they never forget them ; and Japan is always in a state of apprehension. Japan is always afraid that in another moment its mother Nature may lose her temper, and Nature does not often keep Japan long waiting.

For centuries the great artifice of the Japanese Government (or should I say the great art ?) has been to divert the minds of the perpetually frightened Japanese people. The criminal going to the gallows often conserves his personal dignity, and augments his personal courage with a glass of brandy. The Japanese Government holds to the lips of its once-so-often-to-be-by-earthquake-shaken-and-perhaps-destroyed people a cup of redder wine—Blood. The blood of adversaries, or the blood of themselves, seems to be the liquor that, from the earliest history of Japan, has had the greatest power to intoxicate the Japanese people, and to make them forget the sword that hangs above them, and which in any moment may fall and cut into the bowels of their country.

Korea has, of course, been for a very long time

an excuse for war between China and Japan.
They seem to have an uncontrollable appetite for
wrangling with each other, and poor Korea hangs,
like a ready bone, between the open, snarling
mouths of Ah-man and Yamamato.

But, for all that, I verily believe that the immediate causes of the present war in Asia were the
plague in China, and the earthquakes in Japan.
The minds of the Chinese, and the minds of the
Japanese, had to be diverted, else might they both
have gone mad. This is true, at least of Japan,
who struck the first blow, and in many ways
forced the war. Korea has been offered up in
sacrifice by China and Japan, with a devotion to
their own safeties, and a belief in their own gods,
which would have done credit to Abraham. They
poured the vitriol of their hatred over Korea, and
lit her myriad gardens with the torch of war, as
complacently as Moses slew the task-master in the
brick-field of Pharaoh.

Earthquakes are perhaps as little understood as
any of Nature's mysterious phenomena. A new
science has sprung up almost mushroom-like
amongst us of recent years; a science that is
attempting the elucidation to human understand-
ing of the laws that govern earthquakes. This
new science has not as yet made much positive
headway, and seismologists themselves know
comparative little of the phenomena they study.

To-day we are in a Japanese village. In every door-yard great clumps of gorgeous chrysanthemums echo the glory of the sunset, wonderful tangles of wisteria throw their plum-coloured shadows upon the clean white paper windows, and the clean white paper doors of the hundred or more clean little houses. Upon the spotless-floored, flower-wreathed verandahs the waning sunshine sketches in crimson, in purple, and in gold the outlines of the wisteria petals, and the wisteria leaves. Roses, crimson and white and yellow, spot the grass. Painted bowls of blue and white porcelain, heaped with silky rice, stand on the verandahs, and on one verandah, perhaps, stands an old bowl of yellow Satsuma, which holds the evening meal of rice. Lacquered trays of fish stand beside the bowls of rice. The families, soft-featured, pleasing of face, graceful of gesture, gentle of manner, squat artistically upon the spotless floors. The sun sets, the moon comes up, the rice and the fish have been eaten. The birds and the butterflies sing. All is peace and contentment. The beautiful bowls have been tenderly washed, and the villagers have gone to sleep, resting their elaborately dressed heads upon their queer little wooden pillows.

To-morrow we are in the same village, but where is the village ? It is torn and crushed. A thrill has passed through the earth at sunrise

The chrysanthemums shake their heavy heads in terror, the wisteria vines are alive with dismay, every purple head quivering with afright. Every golden bell upon every crimson, lacquered, carved temple cries out in alarm so musical, so sweet, that it is incomprehensible that even so angry, so momentarily relentless a mother as Nature is not moved to pity, and to stay her hand. But no. The wisterias are roughly wrenched from off the walls up which they were wont to climb, decking foot after foot with their lavish beauty. The chrysanthemums are torn into rags so small and pitiful, that if here and there we find an unmutilated petal it seems to us quite huge.

There are few sights more pitiful than the sight of a Japanese village that has been broken by earthquake. Bits of wood, shreds of paper, wrecks of trees, broken flowers, torn vines are tangled together in picturesque, but deplorable *débris*. The people are homeless, at the best, more than probably, they, too, are torn and maimed, most possibly they are killed. The rice is spilled, and the bowls of blue, and white, and of yellow Satsuma are broken. Silver pipes, torn kimonos, bits of pottery, that if whole again were worth a king's ransom, strew the scene, and for the moment hide the gashes in the ground. And yet, like everything else in Japan, even this scene of desolation has its juvenile aspect; it looks not unlike a toy that a spoiled child has broken in anger.

The trouble, the misery, the agony, physical and mental, that earthquakes entail year in and year out on the people of Japan is beyond exaggeration, and quite beyond the pale of light writing. All thinking travellers must feel that it is no wonder that a people periodically subjected to such momentous torture, periodically need a big stimulant. And so, perhaps, it is less shame (than at the first glance it seems) to the powers that in Japan be, that soon after the recent disembowelment of Nagasaki, and the upheaval of many other Japanese states and villages, they, the powerful ones of Japan, have seen fit to go to war with China.

The plague that so recently devastated China, though more repulsive in detail, is far less hopeless to contemplate than the Japanese earthquakes. If China should ever come to the adopting of fairly proper sanitary laws, if China's poverty should ever go down once and for all beneath the iron heel of China's really vast common sense, and China's infinite capacity of contrivance, then would China, always vigorous, be baptized into new health, and then would China's plagues be matters of the past.

I am fain to hope all good things for China. But I fear that earthquakes will never be matters

of the past in Japan. Well, both these peoples—
one very great, the other very charming—have
been sorely afflicted within the last year, and both
have fell a-fighting.

We can only hope that right may prove mighty,
and that in the near end peace may crown the
Asiatic all.

We always think of Japanese women as the
embodiment of everything that is feminine and
gentle. And with the exception of the yoshiwara
and the hardest worked women of the coolie
class, we picture the women of Japan as shrinking
from publicity, from unnecessary exertion, and
from anything bordering on self-assertion. Yet
in the days gone by Japan has had a class of
women who have been quite opposite to all this,
and yet who have been neither yoshiwara nor
coolies. I mean the Japanese Amazons, who have
more than once played active parts in Japanese
warfares. This class has quite died out, but
during the present Chino-Japanese war a number
of Japanese women of high birth have petitioned
the Mikado to permit them to join the army—join
it as active soldiers—at least, so a recent despatch
says. This is funny; but not in the least incredible. The Japanese are the funniest people
alive. They are perpetually doing the most unexpected, I might almost say the most inde-
fensible things, but they do them with such an air

of artistic propriety, that it is a very keen-eyed European indeed who realizes that anything not altogether *au fait,* mentally or morally, has happened.

The Japanese are so incapable of a *gaucherie* that we do not appreciate their very extensive capacity for folly.

A Japanese woman in the thick of the fight! Her kimono well tucked up from her little dimpled feet. Her obi bulging with cartridges! A knapsack rubbing corns on the sweet, stooped, brown shoulders! Armed cap-à-pie! A plumed helmet crushing down the elaborate shape of her perfumed coiffure! A sword hitting roughly against the warm limb, to which bright-eyed, brown children have been wont to gently cling! A great coarse gun chafing the soft arm and softer breast where laughing, yellow babies have slept and dreamed glad, soft dreams, and as they learned to love their mother's milk, learned the three great lessons of Japanese life : learned to be happy, learned to be courteous, learned to be beautiful and artistic! It makes me laugh.

And yet I do not discredit the veracity of the telegram. The Japanese women are very, very drowsy. But when they wake up—and semi-occasionally they do wake up—they wake up with a start.

Great occasions seem to infuse them with electricity. I quite believe that to-day there are in Japan thousands of delicate, daintily accustomed, women who would gladly join the active ranks of war. Japanese patriotism is as supreme, as gracious, as graceful as Japanese art; and unlike Japanese art it is often visionary.

That the Japanese women want to fight the Chinese soldiers—is very amusing, and rather interesting. It proves that they have pluck. It proves that they have bad taste. That it does prove them guilty of bad taste makes it remarkable. The Chino-Japanese wrangle over Korea is, I believe, the first event in all our world's long history that has convicted the women of Japan of bad taste.

Whether any Japanese women would prove effective soldiers, I doubt. I doubt if even the women of the coolie class: the women who sort tea in Kobe, the women who, in Nagasaki, running up and down the sides of P. and O. and other steamers, carry upon their muscular brown backs, murderous loads of coal, would advantageously augment the Japanese army. I doubt if the women of the Ainos (the Ainos are the fiercest, wildest people of Japan) would acquit themselves usefully in the field of battle. That the women of Japan would acquit themselves bravely, nobly, in the terrible moment of battle, admits of no doubt. But to be brave is one thing; to be noble is another; to be useful is still another.

Greatly to his credit (he seems to be—take him all in all—a very worthy, manly sort of fellow), the Emperor of Japan has not, I believe, allowed the women of Japan to swell the pretty ranks of his victorious army.

Yes; the Japanese army is a pretty army. I am speaking disrespectfully of the army of a nation that has beaten the great nation of China! China is not beaten yet. Japan has trod hard, very hard on one of China's toes, and the toe is crushed and bleeding. But China—great big, broad, yellow China is not beaten; and won't be for a few days more.

The Manchu dynasty may be unthroned. But China will go on for hundreds of years very much as she has gone on for hundreds of years. The Japanese army has proved itself a very industrious, capable, workman-like army indeed; but for all that, it is a pretty army.

The Japanese soldiers are plucky little heroes, every one of them, but they look for all the world like toy warriors—toy warriors in nice new uniforms.

If Japan were engaged in war, not with China, but with one of the first-class European Powers, Japan would fight as bravely as she is fighting now, every bit as bravely, but would her success be so swift and meteor-like? I wonder.

If Japan should ever fall a-fighting of a Western power, then I advise the Mikado to enlist as many of his lady subjects as he can, and when the bugle sounds the battle hour, place them in the front ranks. Then might Japan hope to conquer, not one, but every nation in Europe, and have at her feet every army in Christendom. No European soldier could draw sword, or aim gun against the Japanese army, if its front ranks were filled with almond-eyed, smiling-mouthed, crêpe-clad, Amazons. Then would the British soldier cease to sing "God Save the Queen" and "Rule Britannia." Then would he stand at attention before the ranks of Japan; and this the battle hymn he'd sing :—

> " I fear no foe in shining armour
>   Though his lance be swift and keen,
>   But I fear and love the glamour
>   'Neath thy drooping lashes seen."

The Chinese soldier is not so sentimental. He is extremely sensible. "All's game that comes to my gun," is his motto in time of war, and he would argue (not without some show of justice) that if a woman were foolish enough, unsexed enough, to go into the field of battle as a combatant, a maker of carnage, the sooner she were exterminated the better.

Yes; the Emperor of Japan has done well to exclude the dainty women folk of Japan from active participation in the present fray. Let the women of Japan wait. When there is a Japanese-European war, then their turn will have come, and they will have the proud happiness of being Japan's invincible defenders, Japan's strongest soldiers, and the conquerors of all Europe.

A number of Japanese women have petitioned the Emperor to enrol them as army nurses, and send them to the seat of war. So wise a man as Mutsuhito will not, I feel sure, refuse so admirable a suggestion. Cooks are taught sometimes: statesmen made, poets manufactured as often as not. Nurses are born.

The knack of nursing is a gift; a gift from God. Japanese women have this gift to a delightful degree. Physically, they are ideal nurses. Their voices are sweet, low, and clear. Their motion is gentle and graceful. Their touch is cool but comfortable, soft, comforting. They have not a single quality among them that could rasp the sorest nerves.

A Japanese girl (now the wife of a lieutenant in the Japanese navy) used to make illness a perfect treat to me when we were girls at school together. It was a big family ours, almost a thousand, if I remember, but Shige nursed us all, from the Lady Principal to the college cat. We always thought her inspired with a gentle, loving talent for helping and soothing the sick. Certainly she was the best nurse I ever knew: but when I came to live in Japan, I learned that every Japanese woman is an almost ideal nurse.

The Chinese hospitals are hells of horror. The Japanese hospitals are heavens of flower-perfumed rest and consolation.

The soldiers of Japan have acquitted themselves well in the field and in the sea of battle. And they seem to have had all the best of the Korean war.

The woman of Japan will excel always and everywhere in the holier half of war: the binding of wounds, the staunching of blood flow, the decent shrouding of the dead.

And so the strife goes on. The fate of Korea, and perchance the fate of the Far East, hangs in war's awful balance. Yet even now Korea is half asleep amid her lotus-flowers, and far more inclined to dream away a hermit life, hidden behind the Ever-white Mountains, lulled by the crooning of the Yellow and the Japan Seas, than to come out into the tumult, the struggle, and the glare of international day.

THE END.

GLOSSARY.

Ainos—A fierce, almost barbarian people, living in the north of Japan.

Arrack—A strong liquor distilled from rice.

Chulalongkorn—The present king of Siam.

Flower-boats—The boats upon which the Chinese flower-girls live.

Geisha—(Literally) An accomplished person.

Jinrickshaw—A two-wheeled vehicle, pulled by a coolie, or by coolies.

Joss-house—The temple of a Chinese god.

Junks—A species of Chinese boats.

Khan—A partially underground furnace.

Kimono—The principal or outer robe worn both by Japanese men and women.

Ki-saing—A Geisha girl.

Kow-tow—A profound Chinese obeisance.

Lien-hoas—Chinese water-lilies.

Mogree flowers- A peculiarly sweet Indian blossom, worn by the Nautch girls when they dance.

Mutsuhito—The present Emperor of Japan.

Obi—A narrow Japanese belt, worn above a broad sash.

Paddy—Young rice.

Pailow—A Chinese memorial arch, usually erected to the honour of a woman who, upon her husband's death, has killed herself.

X

Purdah-women—Oriental women living in strict family seclusion.

Queue—The long braid of hair worn by Chinese men.

Saki—A strong Japanese liquor.

Sampan—A small, rude, native boat.

Samshu—A Chinese liquor.

Satsuma—A famous Japanese family. A peculiarly beautiful and valuable pottery, especially noted for its glaze, its exquisite decorations, and for its interesting history.

Sen—A small Chinese coin ; a cent ; a hundredth part of a Yen, or dollar.

Son-wang-don—The home of the king of the fairies.

Tai-wan—Formosa.

Taro—A Korean sweet potato.

Torii—A Japanese arch, marking the approach to a temple or sacred place.

Yamun—The official residence of a Chinese mandarin.

Yu-lan—A beautiful flower of the Far East.